LOGAN

A LIFE AFTER COMPANION STORY

BOOK FOUR

JULIE HALL

Julie Hall, www.JulieHallAuthor.com

Cover design by Christian Bentulan

CONTENTS

AWARDS

Winner, Speculative Fiction / *Stealing Embers*
2021 ACFW Carol Awards

Finalist, Paranormal & Supernatural / *Forging Darkness*
2022 Realm Awards

Audiobook Finalist / *Stealing Embers*
2022 Realm Awards

Finalist, Paranormal & Supernatural / *Stealing Embers*
2021 Realm Awards

Finalist, Young Adult / *Stealing Embers*
2021 Realm Awards

Finalist, Readers' Choice / *Stealing Embers*
2021 Realm Awards

Gold Medal Winner / *Stealing Embers*

2021 Illumination Awards

Cover Design Award Finalist / *Huntress*
2021 Realm Awards

Honorable Mention / *Stealing Embers*
2021 Writer's Digest Self-Published Book Awards

Young Adult Finalist / *Stealing Embers*
2020 The Wishing Shelf Book Awards

Finalist, Speculative Fiction / *Huntress*
2018 ACFW Carol Awards

Young Adult Book of the Year / *Huntress*
2018 Christian Indie Awards

Gold Medal Winner / *Huntress*
2018 Illumination Awards

First Place Winner, Religion / *Huntress*
2018 IndieReader Discovery Awards

Christian Fiction Finalist / *Huntress*
2018 Next Generation Indie Book Awards

Alliance Award (Reader's Choice) / *Warfare*
2018 Realm Makers Awards

Parable Award Finalist / *Logan*
2018 Realm Makers Awards

Gold Medal Winner / *Huntress*
2017 The Wishing Shelf Book Awards

Best Debut Author / *Julie Hall*
2017 Ozarks Indie Book Festival

Best Inspirational Novel / *Huntress*
2017 Ozarks Indie Book Festival

Second Place Winner / *Huntress*
2017 ReadFree.ly Indie Book of the Year

First Place Winner / *Huntress*
2012 Women of Faith Writing Contest

USA TODAY **Bestselling Author**
August 17, 2017 & June 21, 2018

To my devoted readers.

I heard you. Your love for the seemingly grumpy mentor with a mysterious past and a bruised heart is what made this book a reality.

This story gives you Logan's perspective and backstory; a view into his trials, his demons, his powers, and his weakness.

INSTRUCTIONS

FOR THE AUTHOR COMMENTARY AND BONUS MATERIAL

You're in for a special treat! This book includes chapter-by-chapter "author commentary" videos, to help you read between the lines and go deeper into the story! At the end of each chapter, go to the web address (URL) or scan the "QR" code and you'll unlock the bonus commentary and material.

How to scan QR codes with an iPhone or iPad:

1. Open the camera app on your iPhone or iPad *(requires iOS 11+)*
2. Hold the device's camera up to the QR code.
3. Your device will automatically recognize the QR code and provide you with an on-screen notification.
4. Tap the notification to be taken to the video.

How to scan QR codes with an Android device:

1. Open the Google Chrome browser.
2. Click on the search/URL box.
3. Click the little square icon that resembles a QR code.
4. Hold the device's camera up to the QR code.
5. Your device will automatically recognize the QR code and provide you with an URL to visit.
6. Press "Go" to be taken to the video.

AUTHOR COMMENTARY

INTRODUCTION

I'm so excited to give you this extra commentary, to help you read between the lines and go deeper into the story! Get started by watching the first video:
JulieHallAuthor.com/logan-intro

LOGAN'S SOUNDTRACK

LISTEN WHILE YOU READ

These handpicked songs perfectly describe Logan. I often
listened to these songs while writing this book. I hope they
inspire you while you read!
JulieHallAuthor.com/logan-playlist

Click "play" or scan the QR code below. You must have a Spotify
account to listen (it's free).

CHAPTER 1

I gritted my teeth as my opponent's blade connected with mine. I was glad the sparring mask I wore hid the effort I had to make. My muscles bunched as I gathered strength to separate our blades, hoping to throw him off balance, but he remained steady on his feet. Still, I had managed to free my weapon and evade his next strike.

Sweat—from both exertion and the stifling nature of the mask —dripped down my face as I traded blows with the warrior in front of me.

Hinges squeaked somewhere behind me, and for a few seconds the sound of rancorous voices and loud jeers from the rec room drowned out the clashing of our blades. Then the room fell quiet again.

Someone had entered the gym.

Curious, I tried to check over my shoulder and lost my footing instead. I shoved the intrusion out of my mind and focused on the task at hand.

Winning this match.

I spotted the swing aimed at my shins from a mile away and

swiftly jumped out of the way, landing a couple of body lengths from where I'd been standing. The sharp gasp that burst from the unwanted spectator almost threw me off my game. Again.

This time I gritted my teeth out of annoyance.

The warrior ran straight at me and we exchanged a series of quick blows. Despite being a friendly sharpening of skills, neither of us was willing to let up. After several years of training, deflecting an attack had become instinctive for me.

I was an experienced hunter, capable of defending Earth's inhabitants against all sorts of evil—evil they neither saw nor accepted. When I fought, whatever weapon I wielded became another extremity, a simple extension of myself. So today my sword was part of my arm—arching, slashing and deflecting with barely a thought.

Where my opponent's advantage lay in his massive size, mine was my speed. As the blade intended for my neck cut through the air, I ducked and rolled out of the way, watching it sail overhead.

I sprang to my feet in one liquid motion.

The challenging-warrior was frustrated so his attacks became sloppy.

I took full advantage of his irritation, so it wasn't long before I had an opening to snap my leg out and hook his right ankle, bringing him to his knees.

If the giant could have seen my face at that moment, the grin I wore would have annoyed him to no end. I was just about to deliver the final blow—which wouldn't actually injure him, but rather signal the end of the match—when someone cleared their throat loud enough that the sound echoed throughout the gym.

A sign that we were not only being watched, but that our playtime had come to an end.

We froze in our positions. No doubt my opponent was just as disappointed by the interruption as I was. He fisted a dagger in his left hand. I almost chuckled. Someone had just foiled his plan for a surprise attack.

Nice try, but I was already two steps ahead of you, my friend.

"Logan, may I have a word with you?"

Ah, Shannon—the kill-joy of the hunter community—and strict mother to all of us lost boys. But what would we do without her?

I took a step back and lowered my sword. "Sure, Shannon. Just give me a sec." I reached down to offer Alrik a hand up, giving it a shake once he was standing, followed by a pat on the back for a job well done.

"Nice try with that dagger there, but I would never have let you get close to me."

Alrik chuckled, the sound muffled beneath his face guard. "That trick would have definitely worked on you half a year ago."

"Yeah, well, half a year ago I was a different person." And wasn't that the truth?

Recognizing he'd hit a sore spot, he changed the subject. "What do you think the Head Mistress over there wants?" He jerked his head in Shannon's direction.

I shrugged. Alrik was always finding new ways of referring to Shannon, knowing full well she could hear him, but not caring in the least.

"Who knows? But if you don't want to get roped into something along with me, you might want to start a speedy retreat."

"Good point."

Heading for the far door, Alrik didn't even bother dematerializing his armor before fleeing. He just gave Shannon a curt nod and was gone.

I started my trek toward her, ridding myself of my armor along the way. It was then that I realized she wasn't alone.

A small female stood with her, positioned almost behind the

stoic angel as if using her for a shield. The girl's eyes zig-zagging across my body in an almost frantic way.

Ah, I thought, *newbie. Must not be used to seeing people materialize and dematerialize things from thin air.*

"Hey, Shannon, what's up?"

I snuck another glance at the girl next to her, keeping my features neutral. She didn't glow, so she was definitely human. Maybe Shannon was taking on an apprentice or something? Getting help with clerical work?

This wisp of a girl couldn't have looked more out of place or uncomfortable in the training gym—my home away from home —if she tried.

I mentally dismissed her as I focused back on the formidable angel in front of me. Girls were the last thing on my mind these days.

"Actually, I've brought you a new trainee."

Hope filled me. A sliver of trepidation slithered through my chest as well, but if they were allowing me to be a mentor again after what happened with Morgan, I must be doing something right.

I'd waited six long months for this day.

I scanned the area behind Shannon but there was only a closed door to the rec room. Maybe she was just giving me a heads up on what was coming down the pipeline soon.

"Oh, yeah? That's great! Where is he?" I asked.

Shannon gave the wisp a gentle shove forward, causing the girl to stumble a bit before righting herself.

"Here *she* is," Shannon answered with a knowing smile.

My usually controlled expression broke. *Oh. Heck. No.*

The widening of my eyes was completely involuntary as I really took stock of this supposed new hunter. Starting at her feet and moving my eyes up her body, I took in every inch of non-hunter in front of me. I'm sure the appraisal had to be uncomfortable, but it couldn't be helped.

She was clearly assigned the wrong job. The top of her head didn't even reach my shoulders. And it wasn't just that she was shorter than any hunter I'd ever met, or even that she was a girl, but she was also incredibly petite in stature as well. Her softly-curved figure also lacked the muscle definition needed for our job. From her tiny feet to her delicate heart shaped face this chick screamed 'damsel in distress,' not 'big bad fighting machine.'

What in the world were they thinking?

I had the crazy urge to bundle her up and whisk her off somewhere safe. There was no way I was going to be able to train this girl.

Her long mane of brown hair matched her large doe eyes, which were glassy at the moment. Oh no, was she going to start crying?

I did not do tears.

I meant to look away, but her eyes wouldn't let me go. I forced words from my mouth. "You have got to be kidding me." I couldn't help the icy bite to my words.

The young girl, who was probably around the age I had been when I'd died, flinched. I instantly regretted my words, but refused to take them back. They were calloused and insulting, but our job—protecting the living from the evil that stalked the Earth —was no joke.

Barely a second passed before Half Pint turned and headed back toward the rec room door, muttering something under her breath the whole way.

Shannon moved faster than either of our eyes could track and the wisp walked right into her, bouncing off the angel, before landing heavily on her butt.

I pressed my lips together tightly to keep the corners from

lifting. Maybe there was a little bit of fight in this wee leprechaun after all?

I was focused solely on the girl until I felt Shannon's gaze on me. When I lifted my eyes, the angel was glowing brightly—a clear sign she was agitated.

Well, if *I* could glow, I'd be a flippin' Lite Brite right now, so she wasn't intimidating in the least.

"You know we don't make mistakes about these things. There's a reason for this."

I ran a hand through my hair and indicated the wanna-be huntress with the other. "She'll be eaten alive out there. Just look at her, Shannon."

A moment of doubt crossed Shannon's face. I saw it and Half Pint probably noticed it as well.

Couldn't they find some nice, safe, more appropriate job for her? Or at least a trainer with a little more patience than I had these days. Even *I* could admit I was a bit of a loose cannon after what went down with Morgan on Earth.

There had to be someone better suited than me.

"Logan, it is what it is," Shannon's voice drew my attention—which had subconsciously drifted to the damsel still sitting on the ground between us—once again, "You've been chosen as her mentor. You need to train her as you would anyone else."

Did that last comment come with a pointed look, or was I just reading too much into it? And then a thought occurred to me.

"Is this because of what happened?" My tone darkened.

"No, Logan, this isn't some sort of punishment. You know things don't work like that here." Shannon paused for a moment. Her features softened and that was almost worse.

I didn't want her pity.

"What do you think they said about Romona when she first joined?"

I looked down at the girl, who in truth wasn't that much smaller than Romona—one of our best fighters—and let out a heavy sigh.

What else could I say?

Shannon knew me well enough to recognize my defeated sigh.

"Thank you, Logan. I'll leave her with you now. You know what to do."

I almost laughed at her words. I had no idea what to do with her.

"Wh-what?" The little sprite had been listening to our conversation with rapt attention, and it appeared that she had just now realized her fate had been sealed—and she wasn't going down without a fight.

I watched silently and with raised eyebrows as she clumsily tried to regain her footing to chase after Shannon. When the door banged shut behind the angel, she stopped and stared. Most likely frozen in disbelief.

I could relate.

Hmm, what's the wisp going to do now?

I was surprised by my own mild interest in this tiny creature. She remained turned toward the door, which gave me a nice view of her—

With a huff, she spun on her heel.

I schooled my features. I had a master poker face. No need for her to know the path my thoughts had taken a moment before.

"Okay," she plopped her hands on her hips and let out a breath. *That absolutely wasn't cute,* I chanted over and over in my head. Maybe if I said it enough it would become true. "So, will you at least tell me what exactly it is that we do?"

I stared straight into her eyes. How could they not have explained her job to her, at least in part? Man, talk about throwing someone right in the deep end. Time to rip off the Band-Aid and see if Half Pint knew how to swim. This chick was in for the shock of her afterlife.

"We kill demons."

She blinked twice. I thought she was going to say something, but instead her eyes rolled back and she dropped to the ground like an anchor hitting the ocean floor.

She was out cold.

———

Author Commentary: Chapter 1
JulieHallAuthor.com/logan-1

CHAPTER 2

TWO AND A HALF YEARS EARLIER

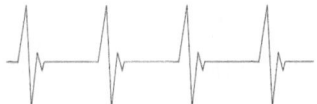

*T*he drink in my hand was tepid and soured in my stomach. To an onlooker, I probably looked wasted. But the glazed expression emanating from my eyes was less from the warm beer I was drinking and more from the thoughts rolling around in my head.

Despite the noise from the beach party around me, the splashing and receding of the surf washing up on shore wouldn't be silenced. Salty waves beat against the beach again and again only to be sucked back into the vast ocean. The sand would either be covered in water during high tide, or dried out by the sun's rays at low tide.

Underwater or dried out. That's exactly how I felt these days.

This party was like any other I'd gone to during high school. Booze, drugs, music, and filled with over-exaggerated everything. Loud laughing, sloppy dancing, and poor decisions we all blamed on the booze, drugs or music the next day and just moved on.

Everything was the same, except this time the only difference was me.

But no one seemed to care and I couldn't drum up the emotion to care that they didn't care.

An ocean breeze blew my shaggy hair around my head and with it the smell of brine and warm beer. I hadn't drunk that much, but there was a chance I was still going to be sick.

What am I still doing here?

Just as I was about to get out of the lounge chair I'd taken possession of for the last half hour—the one I'd pointed at the water rather than the festivities—a body plopped into my lap, sloshing the warm drink on both of us.

I let out an annoyed growl as I dumped the remainder of my cheap beer into the sand before it could do anymore damage. My mind more on thoughts of how it was going to stink up my car than the drunken girl trying to straddle my lap.

In her quest, she elbowed me in the gut and my annoyance turned to her.

"Oops, sorry Logan," she said before dissolving into a fit of giggles that brought her stale breath and unfocused gaze closer to my chest. I restrained myself from standing up and dumping her on her butt into the sand. I knew Rachel. We went to the same school and under normal circumstances she wasn't nearly this . . . annoying. I told myself she was just having a good time and I shouldn't bring her down. But I was done with this party tonight. Maybe done for a while.

"Hey, what's up with you? Whatcha doin' sitting over here all by yourself?" she asked after she regained some semblance of composure.

She wasn't wrong. This wasn't my usual M.O. for these parties. I was often one of the loudest and most annoying of them all. But something just wasn't sitting right with me these days and it couldn't be ignored anymore.

"Just feeling more like chilling tonight, I guess," I answered, trying hard not to stare at the ample amount of cleavage on display, exactly at eye-level.

"I could be up for chillin'." Rachel's attempt at casual seduction was anything but. There was nothing subtle about her literally throwing her body at me. Her eyes weren't half closed with desire, but rather due to whatever drinks or pills she'd consumed that night.

That was not hot.

I fought against another wave of irritation that called for me to shove her body harshly off of mine.

What was wrong with me?

In the past, this would have been the type of scenario I would have been down for. Rachel was cute; I'd never cared how much someone else was under the influence before going for it. Heck, I was usually just as plastered as they were and sometimes didn't remember much the next day, but right now, I was just disgusted. Not at Rachel, but at myself.

Is this really how I want to go through my life?

I gently, but firmly, removed her hands from my shoulders and then lifted her off my lap as I stood up. She teetered on her feet and giggled some more as she used my body to keep her own upright. I gritted my teeth and waited for her to regain at least some of her balance before removing her hands from me once again.

"I'm gonna head out." I jerked my chin towards the parking area up the way to indicate that I meant I was going to leave the party, not just leave her. I was never one to needlessly hurt people's feelings, but if this chick didn't get the hint soon, it might come to that.

Something was roiling inside my gut, screaming at me to run from this place. Itching to get out of there, I was little more than a ticking time-bomb, unsure of when the countdown would reach zero. When I exploded I wanted to be far away from this place.

"Aw, come on, Logan. Don't be like that. It's not even late. You can't leave yet." She jutted her lip out into an exaggerated pout. Did girls think that was attractive?

Rachel made a move to latch on to me again but I quickly side-stepped and took off. I think she landed on the lounge chair because of the racket behind me, but I refused to turn around to check. I was *so* done.

Long strides took me closer to my car. And each step away from the party lifted some of the pressure in my chest, making me feel lighter somehow.

"Hey, handsome, where are you headed off to?" The clear and crisp nature of her words and familiarity of her voice tempered my need to flee. Kaitlin was just getting out of her lime-green VW Bug Convertible when I reached the rows of parked cars. My black Mustang was a few cars down from hers, but the itch to reach it lessened for a moment.

"Just not feeling it tonight, I guess," I answered. Kaitlin's quintessential California girl look with her blonde hair pulled up into a high ponytail, tanned skin, and athletic build was probably an exact match for my laid-back surfer persona. I'm sure lots of people assumed we were a *thing* at one time or another. But it had never been that way between the two of us.

I'd known Kaitlin for practically my whole life. In a weird way, she was the closest thing I had to a sibling. We'd bonded over who-knows-what sometime along the way and now we watched out for each other.

Her eyes narrowed and her brow pinched. I braced myself for a round of twenty questions, silently cursing the wind as I shoved the hair from my face, and waited for her to come up with the first one. Clearly, we knew each other a little too well.

Kaitlin was probably the only girl here I wouldn't blow off if pushed too far. Maybe that was wrong, but it was the truth.

Her slow nod spoke of understanding and I almost dropped my jaw at her next comment.

"Yeah, I get where you're coming from." She looked out over the beach where the bonfire blazed. From up here under the lights, you couldn't see much down past the circumference of the fire's light. "These things don't seem as exciting as they used to, do they?"

I opened my mouth to respond but no sound came out.

Kaitlin didn't wait for me to speak. "I'm just gonna pop in myself and say hi to a few people before heading out too," her gaze jerked back to me, "You haven't been drinking have you? You're okay to drive?"

I ignored her first question and answered the second. "Yeah, I'm good to drive. You have fun. I'll see you later."

She nodded her approval—probably assuming I was confirming the not-drinking-anything question—and I waved a quick goodbye.

I was fine to drive, so she didn't need to know I'd had a few drinks of beer in me. Really only one because the second barely counted. I wore more of it than I had actually drank. *Thank you very much, Rachel.*

I reached my car a moment later and breathed a sigh of relief. Something was seriously wrong with me.

I started the muscle car and enjoyed the rumble of the engine before carefully reversing and pulling out onto PCH—Pacific Coast Highway ran north and south along most of the pacific coast of California—leaving the festivities behind.

Both literally and figuratively.

I carefully maneuvered my car around the bends and turns in the road because although I felt like I was one hundred percent okay to drive, I still didn't want to be caught by a cop. Being underage at eighteen, any number that popped up on a breathalyzer would be too high. So, regardless of how fast I might push it during the day, my hands remained firmly at the ten-and-two position as I carefully made my way home.

But that restless mind of mine just wouldn't shut up and I found myself pulling off at one of the scenic overlooks along the road. It was a favorite late-night spot of mine because it was far enough away from the city to see the stars, and hidden enough that it was hard to find. The singular deterrent was the occasional car that did stumble across my hidden oasis to use it for a different sort of privacy. Tonight it was blessedly empty when I pulled off the road. I got out of the car and hopped up on the hood so I could lean back and gaze upon the heavens.

It was a cloudless night, so the cosmos was out, its full glory on display. I could even see the edge of the Milky Way, like a dusting of freckles set upon the darkened sky.

I inhaled a deep breath of salty air and was warmed by the metal beneath me as a cool breeze washed over my body. Even though most of my clothes had dried since their earlier beer bath, the faint smell still infused the air around me when the wind died down. It was washed away with every new gust of air off the Pacific, only to return between breaks.

I was going to have to be extra careful to get these clothes in the wash before my parents woke up in the morning. I'm sure they already suspected what I was doing when I went out with my friends, but no point in giving them any reason to get on my case when I hadn't even done anything this time.

Thoughts of the party slowly leaked from my brain as I continued to stare at the expanse above. For the last few years, my life had consisted of three main things: surfing, parties, and girls. But lately, deep life questions had begun to haunt me, making me feel much older than I truly was.

What was I doing with my life? Where was I going? Was I making a difference in the world? Did I even care if I did?

My mind was a cluttered mess. I beat down the uncertainty and let all thoughts fly from my head on a loud exhale. A perfect moment of silence followed as I watched a star streak across the sky. I gulped in the ocean breeze and a question bigger than myself trickled into my subconscious.

Could all of this beauty in the world really have been put here by accident? What if there was something bigger at work?

"My will, not yours."

Those words echoed in my brain in an unnatural way.

I jack-knifed into a sitting position and turned my head from side to side making sure I was truly alone.

Had I actually heard those words . . . or was I hallucinating now? Had someone slipped something into the one drink I'd had?

My gaze was prowling the surrounding area for the person who had spoken when I was momentarily blinded by a set of headlights.

Great, my reprieve was over. Might as well head home, I guess.

I slid off the hood of my car and was about to open the driver's side door when the short *whoop* of a police siren froze me in my tracks.

I yanked my guilty hand from the door handle as if it had been burned. I couldn't get in trouble if they hadn't actually caught me driving, could I?

As I turned, the police cruiser came to a stop in the spot next to my own.

I groaned silently as a door opened, then slammed shut.

This was just great. I should have just stayed home tonight.

I turned my body and leaned up against the side of the car, crossing my arms over my chest. Might as well find out what the cop wanted. I'd been here too long for him to have followed me under suspicion of drinking and driving, but the second I got behind that wheel he could slap me with a DUI *and* underage drinking charge.

No thank you.

An older man with salt-and-pepper streaked hair came around the front of his standard issued police cruiser. He reminded me of my dad for some reason. Maybe it was the man's athletic build—despite being past his prime—or perhaps it was just the air of authority cops gave off in general.

Whatever the reason, I shook it off and forced a neutral expression on my face.

"Everything okay out here, son?" the officer asked.

My knee jerk reaction was to tell him I wasn't his son, but that wasn't going to land me anywhere I wanted to be.

"Yeah, I'm good." Short and to the point. Why offer any more information than was necessary?

His eyes, although not hostile, remained locked on my face. I returned his stare hoping it sent him the I've-got-nothing-to-hide vibe.

"Well, that's good to hear. I happened to see a car parked here on my way back to the station and just wanted to check to make sure everything was okay. Glad to see no one has any car trouble."

I almost snorted. Yeah, he was probably checking to make sure no one was getting it on, was more like it.

"Nope. The car is fine, sir, just doing some star gazing to clear my head."

This guy wasn't a fool, but it didn't appear like he was looking for trouble either.

He nodded at me and cracked a small smile. The gesture seemed friendly, but what did I know? I didn't have much experience with cops.

He could check my car if he wanted. He wasn't going to find anything incriminating in there.

"Well, then," he began, "seeing that everything is alright here, I'll just be on my way."

At that moment, the wind shifted and blew my beer-drenched scent directly at the cop.

The officer stopped in his tracks and turned back toward me. His gaze wasn't as friendly as it had been a moment before.

Not moving a muscle, I remained casually leaning against my driver's side door with my arms folded across my chest. My face held the same look that I was sure gave nothing away. But I did hold my breath and sent up a silent prayer to whomever was out there that this guy would just turn back around and drive off.

My prayer went unanswered.

"Did you drive this car out here tonight, son?"

I was not this guy's son. And what could I say to that? There wasn't anyone else around, so a lie wouldn't have been convincing.

"Yes, sir."

"And have you been drinking tonight?" He didn't beat around the bush.

Lie or truth? Which one would get me in less trouble? Because right now this cop was like a dog with a bone.

"Someone spilled their drink on me. That's what you smell, officer. That's why it's so strong." Half-truth and evasion, it was.

This guy wasn't an idiot, so I knew he would be able to tell right away that I wasn't drunk. But I also didn't look twenty-one, and I smelled like a brewery.

My only hope was that he'd take my word for it or let me off with a slap on my wrist. I got underage drinking was illegal, but come on, didn't everyone do it? And he had to actually catch me driving to slap me with a DUI, right? But I'd just admitted to having driven the car here myself.

Shoot.

———

Author Commentary: Chapter 2
<u>JulieHallAuthor.com/logan-2</u>

CHAPTER 3

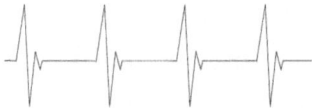

"*Y*ou know getting off with only community service for the rest of the year is actually pretty lucky."

I cracked my neck and shot Kaitlin an irritated look. She wasn't wrong, but the whole ordeal was a mess and I would never hear the end of it from my parents. They'd had to pick me up at the police station. The lectures hadn't stopped since, and they'd revoked my 'car privileges' for the next month.

I slammed my locker shut and walked down the hall without responding to Kaitlin. I was being a jerk; it certainly wasn't her fault I was arrested for underage drinking. I was lucky they hadn't stuck me with a DUI charge as well. They certainly could have because it was obvious that I had driven the car to the overlook.

I was eighteen and about to graduate from high school, and hated being treated like a child. It rubbed me the wrong way.

Bumming rides off friends was a real pain.

But not only that, the feeling of 'off-ness' still hadn't gone away. It nagged and picked at me daily.

"Hey, wait up!" Kaitlin called after me. I slowed my gait.

"Come on, Logan. I know you. There's something else bothering you."

I arched a brow. She wasn't wrong. She knew me well enough to pick up on that fact, but she also should have known I wasn't big on talking about my feelings and such. I liked to work stuff out on my own. Even though Kaitlin and I were close, the number of times I had actually confided in her about deeper issues was minimal.

"Are you being serious, right now?" I asked.

She gave me a playful shove. "Don't give me that look. I know I'm right, and it isn't something that just came up. You've been acting . . . different, for a while now. Something is bothering you. I can tell." She narrowed her eyes and went up on her toes, and forcefully grabbed my head, tilting it side to side as if she was searching for something buried in my hair.

"Hey, cut it out," I swatted her away, "What the heck are you doing?"

"Yep, it's just as I feared." *What was this chick talking about?* "The gears in there are definitely turning, but they're a little rusty and covered in cobwebs, so it's taking you extra long to work it out. You are in obvious need of a good friend, right now."

I barked out an involuntary laugh before rolling my eyes at her. "You're a weirdo, you know that?"

She shrugged, her smile still in place. "Takes one to know one."

"Whatever." Sometimes there was nothing to do but shake your head at Kaitlin. "I'm headed to class." A few more weeks until I was out of here, then I could concentrate on my surfing career full time.

That was another point of contention with my parents. I wanted to go pro, and they wanted me to go to college instead. I'd been accepted to several schools. Between my decent grades and my surfing skills I had even snagged a few privately-funded scholarships for student athletes.

I'd been competing in the juniors for years . . . and yeah, I may be jumping the gun a little early by trying to go pro right out of high school, but I at least wanted to give it a shot.

My parents' argument was to go to college and spend the time getting a degree and perfecting my sport, but I didn't want to waste four years when I could be doing what I loved every day.

Before I could leave, Kaitlin grabbed my arm, her expression morphing into one that rarely graced her face . . . seriousness sprinkled with a dose of uncertainty.

"Hey, do you think we could talk sometime? Even if you don't want to open up—I get that, by the way—but there has been some stuff I've been thinking about lately and I wanted someone to . . ." she lifted and dropped a single shoulder, "I don't know, I guess just someone I trusted I could talk to it about."

My body drained of all levity as my concern for Kaitlin rose. I grasped her shoulders and turned her to face me fully. She wouldn't look me in the eyes as she played with the end of her ponytail.

"Kaitlin, what's wrong?" My voice had dropped an octave. If someone was messing with her, they were in for a world of hurt. A shiver of fear ran through me at the thought that she might be in some sort of trouble. I ignored it as I waited for her to answer.

She heaved a sigh before finally meeting my gaze. "It's nothing like what you're thinking, Logan. I'm fine, really. In fact . . ." she paused and her brows pinched as she chose her next words, "for the first time everything might actually be . . . right."

Confused I tilted my head like a puppy trying to interpret its owner's words. And then she laughed.

Laughed. In. My. Face.

Was she messing with me right now? If so, I was never going to take anything she said seriously again.

"I'm sorry, Logan. Your expression right now . . . it's just priceless." She hiccuped, and then slapped a hand to her mouth to stop any more noise from escaping.

"Hey, you two, get a room already!" someone down the hall yelled. The comment was followed by a couple of hoots and inappropriate remarks.

I rolled my eyes. We got random junk like that all the time. Just because we looked like we'd make a cute couple or whatever, didn't mean it was ever going to happen. She was like a sister to me.

Kaitlin scrunched her nose in disgust, mirroring my thought. If I hadn't felt the same I might have been offended.

"That's gross."

I grabbed my chest as if I'd been shot. "Ouch. You mean you *don't* want to get a room with me? That hurts. Haven't you heard? I'm irresistible," I said with a wink.

"I repeat, gross. Maybe if I hadn't seen you eat your boogers in middle school you might be marginally attractive to me, but yeah, no. That's never happening."

A roar of laughter rose in my chest and escaped my lips.

"I'm a guy, Kaitlin. We all do gross stuff at one time or another. It's a given."

"Yeah, well, that pretty much sealed the deal for me. You," she finished her statement with a pointed finger in my face, "are forever planted in the friend zone."

I chuckled at our banter since it put me in a better mood, all of our heavy talk forgotten for the moment. Messing with Kaitlin was a fun sport of mine. I tossed an arm around her neck and led her in the direction of both of our first-period classes.

"Don't let my adolescent behaviors get around. I got a rep with all the ladies to uphold."

"Yes," Kaitlin deadpanned, "I'm very aware of your rep."

Nothing like a good friend to keep your ego in check.

———

"Say something," Kaitlin pleaded with both her eyes and words.

"You . . . found God?" I shifted awkwardly in the too small plastic chair. Being after school, we had the library basically to ourselves. I cast a quick glance around just to make sure no one had overheard Kaitlin's confession. I didn't want to make her feel weird, but her admission had been a little out there, even for me. I'd prepared myself to sit through an emotional monologue about her failed attempts at snagging some guy . . . boy, was I wrong.

"Don't say it like that. You make it sound like I've joined a cult or something."

"Well . . . *have* you?" I widened my eyes unnaturally large, "Wait, did you drink any funny-smelling Kool-Aid while you were at one of those meetings?"

"Gosh, Logan. No! Geez, dramatic much?"

I lifted my hands up in defense. Truth was I didn't know what to say, so I resorted to jokes. What Kaitlin had just described to me poked at that spot inside I'd been trying to ignore. The itchy feeling was back and something about this conversation made me really uncomfortable, and I was using humor to hide it.

"Look, it's not like I'm trying to convince you of anything. I just wanted to tell you what's been going on with me."

Kaitlin's shoulders hunched and she played with the end of her ponytail, something she often did when nervous. Her eyes were downcast. Everything in her posture spoke of vulnerability and here I was cracking jokes to cover my own conflicted heart.

I took in a huge breath of air and let it out slowly, then ran a hand through my hair, not caring in the least the crazy directions I sent it.

"Hey," I laid a gentle hand on her shoulder, "I'm sorry for making light of this. I just don't . . ." It was my turn to look for the right words, but they were missing. "I just don't know what to say."

A weak smile touched Kaitlin's lips. "You don't need to say anything, okay? I just wanted an ear to listen."

I could do that for her. "Okay. Whenever you want to talk about this stuff, I promise I'll listen. I may not get what's going on with you right now, but I can be that friend."

"Thanks, Logan," she leaned forward and gave me a quick squeeze, "I'd better head to practice now. I'll see you later, okay?"

I forced a wide smile. "Yep, definitely."

An hour after Kaitlin left I was still sitting in the same chair, running over everything she'd said.

———

"Give me a break, Logan," Kaitlin's eyes, as well as her words, held a world of skepticism, "Like you never thought all of this could be part of a bigger design." Her hand swept wide to indicate the world around us.

We were hanging out in my favorite spot. Or rather ex-favorite spot. Getting arrested for the first time in a location kind of steals the luster away. We watched the ocean's waves tumble and roll toward shore. Salty mist would irritate my nose a few moments after each large wave crashed against the cliff beneath us.

"I don't buy it," Kaitlin continued, "I've seen you deep in thought enough—especially these last few months—to know that something else besides 'girls' is rolling around that dusty shell you call a brain."

I scoffed. "We both know my brain is very high functioning —" I was cut off by Kaitlin's own scoff, "What? Would you like to compare SAT scores?"

She sealed her lips and narrowed her eyes in mock anger.

"And I think you're severely underestimating the amount of time guys spend thinking about girls."

"You're probably right about that second one."

"And the first?"

"Oh, shut it!" she said and smacked my mid-section. Laughter rumbled from my gut.

"Don't be a hater."

She rolled her eyes and I knew we were on safer ground. She was right. Some of the things she had been talking about these last few months had started to make a little too much sense to me. We'd graduated a few weeks back and after many arguments with my parents, I was about to start my run to become a pro-surfer. So, I don't even know why I was giving Kaitlin's talks a second thought.

I had agreed to be a sounding board—it was the least I could do as her friend—but that was it. Somewhere along the way a God of the universe didn't sound quite as crazy as it had when she had first brought it up to me. And now that didn't just make me uncomfortable, it scared me on a level even *I* didn't understand.

All it would take would be to let go of my old beliefs, and embrace what was starting to resonate as truth . . . but I wasn't ready to pry my fingers loose quite yet. I didn't want anything to derail the plans I had for the future. Even if that meant ignoring the changes stirring inside my heart.

———

Three months into the pro-surfing circuit and it was exactly how I had expected it to be. Which left me feeling exactly how I *hadn't* expected to feel.

Hollow.

I lay on my board, staring into the cloudless blue Hawaiian skies as I bobbed in the water past the break. My body moved up and down to the lazy rhythm of the ocean as the coolness of the water on my backside warred with the Pacific sun's rays beating down on me from above.

It was still too early in the fall to worry about sharks migrating up from the south, not that sharks were ever a big concern of mine. For the most part you left them alone, and they left you alone. With arms stretched out on either side, I probably appeared to be a juicy snack to any great white. But my mind wasn't really focused on any of that. Instead, it was rolling around making friends with that hollow feeling inside.

It made no sense. The surfing was amazing. Yeah, the competition was intense, but I lived for that kind of stuff. I enjoyed the challenge and constant drive to excel, adrenaline pumping in my veins, my focus crystal clear. Almost nothing else could compare to being out in the free, wild waters where I was one with the ocean.

Most of the other surfers were cool guys, so no complaints there. The parties . . . well they were as unbelievable as I'd expected. So again, no surprises. And the girls . . . ah . . . yeah, the girls were also something I expected would come with going pro. I'd never had trouble in that department before, but I didn't like the feeling that I was a commodity to them now. Even though I was new to the major leagues of this sport, the girls looked at me like their meal ticket now . . . or at the very least a bragging right.

I watched other surfers use what was freely offered to them and consider it a perk of the sport, but something about it didn't sit well with me anymore. No one around me seemed to care the way I did. Part of me longed for the oblivion I had lived in before, even if I now saw it for what it was . . . simply chasing after the wind. A poor imitation of something that was supposed to hold more meaning.

For the millionth time, I wondered what exactly was going on with me. There was only one thing for certain; something needed to change.

I was straddling a fence refusing to pick a side, and it made my life grayer by the day.

I was currently in off-season training. Technically speaking, surfing was a year-around sport. The athletes simply chased the warm weather and the waves. After getting my feet wet in the pros so soon after graduation, I had decided to take a short break from competition to get ready for the official winter season to start. There were lots of surfers who did the same, so I was still surrounded by the community and lifestyle. Currently in a lull between tournaments, I used this time to train where the next big tournaments would start to pick up again.

I kept loose track of some of my friends from high school via one form of social media or another, but for the most part, I knew those friendships probably wouldn't last much longer. Except for Kaitlin, who reached out over calls or texts on a weekly basis, mostly with updates on her life at UCLA where she'd joined the volleyball team as a walk-on. But, sometimes she'd ask me deeper questions about how I was doing. I considered ignoring some of her messages, though years of friendship and loyalty refused to let me.

Some vital part of me had begun to change so many months ago, and I tried my hardest to ignore the constant scratch that pestered me. I kept telling myself to move on, that it would go away with time. But more and more my conversations with Kaitlin crept back into my consciousness. No amount of shoving them to the recesses of my mind would keep them buried any longer. And that annoyed me to no end.

I was due for a trip home in a few weeks and I knew there was a reunion party brewing already. *Ha!* Reunion party for people who had been apart for less than six months seemed silly to me, but I promised Kaitlin I'd be there, so I would.

If only this restlessness would leave me. I just wanted . . . peace.

"Be still, and know that I am God."

I sat up so fast I dumped myself right off my board. Some pro-surfer I was. I surfaced quickly and coughed to free my lungs of the briny water I'd inhaled, and then grabbed my board with one arm as I looked around the ocean to see who had spoken.

What was that?

It was just like the night I'd been stargazing, before I'd gotten arrested. A voice that sounded clear as day, but echoed in my head instead of the air around me. This time I couldn't blame it on the possibility of a hallucinogenic dropped in my beer. Despite the ease of availability these days, I actually hadn't had a sip of alcohol in months.

I was stone cold sober.

So, there were two explanations here. Either my mind was playing tricks on me, or there really was someone—or something—out there trying to talk to me. The grip on my old life just tightened a little more. I was getting off of this fence, today, and I knew exactly how to do it.

———

Six hours later, I was exactly where I told myself I wanted to be. Sitting poolside, with my vision just the right amount of hazy, a bikini-clad brunette at my side. I had always had a thing for brunettes, who really knew why.

I was young and attractive . . . heck, I was a pro-athlete. This was exactly how I was supposed to be living my life.

Correction, this is exactly how I was supposed to be enjoying my life.

Then why aren't you enjoying yourself right now? My mind whispered defiantly. I told myself to shut it.

"What was that, baby?" asked the almost-naked girl at my side.

Dang. Had I said that out loud? I must be drunker than I'd thought.

"Nothing." I waved her off and she shrugged in response.

After a few minutes, her arm skated across my naked chest. I told myself that it felt nice, not that it made my skin crawl.

"So, Jace said that there were some guest bedrooms upstairs. Want to go check one of them out with me?"

Shocker, another girl who lacked a subtle bone in her body. But I was doing this. I was shaking off the doubts that had plagued me for months and robbed me of the fun I should be having. This was exactly the type of night I had been expecting when I had shown up to this party.

I shot the girl a cocky grin and simply lifted my chin to let her know I was down. What was her name again? I honestly couldn't remember. Maybe she didn't remember mine either, and that's why she'd called me 'baby' before. I told myself it didn't matter.

We both got up, me a little less graceful than was normal—I'd lost count of the shots I'd taken that evening—and walked into the house, the girl leading the way because I didn't have any idea where Jace's guest bedrooms were. I barely even knew Jace.

She stopped in front of a door and turned to send me a sly

smile over her shoulder. It looked more creepy than seductive to me, but what did I know? I was wasted, and committed to the course of action.

She opened the door and beckoned me in. I watched with glassy eyes as she moved her hands up to untie the top of her swimsuit. I had a vague thought that I should be more excited about this, but shoved it away.

Just as she was about to untie the strings that would cause her top to drop away, something in my stomach turned. And I didn't mean that in a metaphorical sense. I meant that in an, 'I'm-gonna-blow' sense.

My stomach's revolt must have shown on my face because she stopped short and sent me a confused look, brows scrunched and upper lip pulled north.

"Um, are you feeling alright there, babe?" Yep, she definitely didn't remember my name.

I made an attempt to laugh it off. Like I was going to let an upset stomach ruin my night. "Yeah, I'm totally—" I couldn't even make it through the sentence before vomit spewed from my mouth, as if someone had forcefully squeezed my stomach, causing the alcohol mixed with bits of food to project right onto the brunette and her pristine white, barely-there bikini. It slid down all her ample curves. Suddenly, they weren't as attractive as they'd been a minute before.

We both stood motionless for a beat before the girl began to scream in disgust. She fled the room, and I ran for the door that I prayed would lead me to the bathroom.

It *was* the bathroom. Finally, something was going right. Or as right as it could, because I continued to vomit and heave into the porcelain toilet for at least another fifteen minutes until nothing else came up.

Perhaps I should have been embarrassed by what had just

happened, but after the alcohol was ejected from my body —*nothing like a good puke to sober a guy up*—I realized more than anything, I was relieved. And that was all sorts of backwards.

I knew I was too messed up to drive, so after I stopped dry heaving I drank as much water from the tap as I could keep down, and stumbled out of Jace's house and onto the beach. The one place I always felt at home. I walked a short distance before dropping to the damp sand, hanging my head between my arms.

I'd changed. I was still changing. And I was finally ready to let go.

Author Commentary: Chapter 3
JulieHallAuthor.com/logan-3

CHAPTER 4

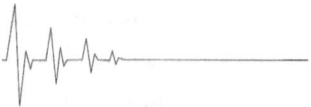

"You're actually here!" Kaitlin's scream slapped me in the face the moment I opened the car door. I'd barely unfolded my long legs from the bucket seat of Reeve's sports car to stand to my full height before a blonde bundle of energy slammed into me.

My back hit the side of the car as I absorbed the impact. Thank goodness, I'd positioned myself a little to the side or we both would have fallen back inside the car. She hadn't even given me the chance to close my door.

"Hey, Kaitlin," I chuckled as I squeezed her and then returned her to her feet, "It's good to see you too."

The smile on her face couldn't have been brighter. It was so wide I was pretty sure she was showing off a few molars at the moment.

"Let me check." She tilted her head to the side and twisted it back and forth as she ran her over-exaggerated gaze from head to toe and back again, bobbing up and down as she went. One of her eyes was closed and the other was squinted as if she was examining me. Something about the way she moved reminded me of a baboon.

"Cut that out." I forced her to stop and shot her an annoyed look.

"Yep, there's definitely something different about you." Her mega-watt smile was back.

"Give me a break." I rolled my eyes at Kaitlin. That night on the beach, several weeks ago, after I'd vomited on the chick I was looking to score with—whose name I still didn't recall—something had happened. I'd finally let go of my old life and put my trust in someone greater than myself. I'd called—perhaps mistakenly—Kaitlin the next day to tell her what had happened. There was lots of squealing involved on her side of the phone.

It's not as if everything had changed overnight, but some things had. That itchy restlessness I'd been struggling with for months had finally quieted. And I had something I didn't before —hope.

"Welcome to the club, little brother."

"Little?" I arched a brow and tilted my head to look down. It wasn't as if Kaitlin was short, she was actually quite tall . . . for a girl. But my six-three height gave me at least four or five inches on her.

"Yep, my birthday is two months before yours. That makes you the little sibling."

"If you say so."

"What club?" Reeve asked. He was a buddy from high school who'd given me a lift that evening. His parents had just bought him a new Camaro Z28 for having made it through his first few months of college without being kicked out, and he was looking to show it off tonight.

"Nothing," I answered, "Ignore the annoying blonde in front of me. She just likes to hear herself talk."

"Hey! That's not true," She turned her attention to Reeve with a gleam in her eye that caused an involuntary groan to crawl up my chest. She was about to say something to embarrass me. I could feel it. "I'll have you know Logan has some pretty big news. A few weeks ago—"

I slapped my hand over her mouth, stopping whatever words were trying to make their way out of that devious head of hers. I did a quick check of her clothes to make sure I wouldn't be causing any indecent exposure, bent Kaitlin under my arm and picked her up, removing the hand from her mouth to keep a strong grip on her while I strode towards the group of our high school friends.

"Logan Barron London, you put me down right now."

Uh-oh, she'd just used my full name. Was that supposed to be intimidating?

I chuckled.

"Listen up, you. I know some defensive skills that could take away your ability to have kids someday. You drop me right now!"

Ouch.

An involuntary wince overtook my body, wiping the cocky grin from my face. You don't joke about things like that. If that was how she wanted to play it, fine.

"You want to be dropped? No problem."

I released my hold on a squirming Kaitlin, making sure I crouched so that her fall to the sand wasn't far, and listened as she sputtered when the surf rode up the shore and knocked into her.

"Logan!"

I turned and continued walking backwards. A full-on belly-laugh burst free. It started in my gut then moved up to my chest. She scurried out of the water's path on her hands and knees. The glare she shot me promised retribution. I didn't doubt for a second that one day I'd be paying for that sin.

When she finally got to her feet, the left half of her body was covered in wet sand and her once perfectly straightened hair was a tangled mess. She assessed her condition as if she couldn't believe what had just happened.

Another bark of laughter from me drew her attention.

The smile she shot me was nothing short of chilling. It said she already had a plan of retaliation brewing in her head. That look alone should have given me cause for pause, but I just laughed louder and waved her over.

"Come on, Kaitlin. You're missing all the fun."

She stuck her tongue out at me in the perfect sibling gesture before jogging to catch up, and then punching me in the arm when she had.

"That was sneaky. You know I'm gonna get you back for that."

"Oh yes, I'm aware. Now let's go say hi to all of our old classmates."

"You're lucky there's no one here I'm looking to impress." She brought a hand up to the soggy side of her head and tried to finger comb through her now-matted hair.

"Hey, I just did you a favor."

"Oh, yeah? How do you figure?"

"The lucky guy who ends up with you should think you're beautiful even at your worst."

She returned the eye roll I gave her earlier.

"Okay, Mom. Thanks." Sarcasm dripped from her voice.

"Mom? I can honestly say that's the first time anyone has called me that." I curled my upper lip, "Yuck. Hopefully the last as well."

"Oh, new nickname for you. I like!" Kaitlin clapped with glee.

"Hey look, Logan's here!" someone yelled, cutting off our conversation, "The party has finally arrived." A round of cheers went up from the rather large group around us.

Apparently, quite a few of my old classmates were trying to relive their high school glory days. And even though I'd been more subdued in my attendance and participation of parties those last few months of school, my reputation as a partier was still locked down.

Well, I thought to myself, *this ought to be an interesting experience.*

———

I kept a bottle of water in my hand the entire night to keep people from shoving red solo cups at me. It helped a little, but it still seemed like every third person was trying to get me to drink that evening. Especially the girls. Something about me not partaking in recreational drinking seemed to make people nervous.

I'd gotten more than one strange look each time I'd declined an invitation, whether it was for a drink or something more. At one point in the night I'd happened to accidentally catch Rachel's eye, the girl I'd turned down all those months ago. *Whoops!* She quickly looked the other way and disappeared into a group of her friends. What might have been a twinge of regret pinched my chest. Not regret for having turned her down, but for having caused her embarrassment in the process.

I'd done my fair share of embarrassing things in a drunken haze—something I hoped was in my past—but I knew it was different for girls. Personally, I'd just groaned about it the next morning and then pretty much forgot it ever happened. Girls seemed to take these types of things harder. It was somewhat of a mystery to me, but I guess there were some areas in which we truly were different.

I'd never cared before what a girl might have felt like after making a fool of herself, but now I did. That alone was proof of the change happening within me. I steered clear of her for the rest of the night. Talking with me would not lessen her embarrassment, and I also wasn't looking for a repeat of that evening.

I used to call most of the people around me friends, but in reality, they were more like acquaintances. When all you had in common with someone was that you liked to party together, you weren't truly friends. I hadn't seen the difference before, but I did now.

Everyone wanted to know what it was like to be a pro-surfer. I'd been an excellent surfer in high school, but skipping college to go straight pro was something of a novelty. The guys wanted to know about all the perks, and they didn't mean the endorsements. They wanted the nitty-gritty details on the girls and parties. Something I was uncomfortable talking about.

As the night went on, the girls got bolder and sloppier in their pursuit of me, some latching themselves on to my arms as they tried to hold a conversation with me even as they slurred their words. So not attractive.

"Hey, Mr. Popular." Kaitlin slid up next to me body-checking one of the girls away. I pretended not to notice.

"Hey, yourself. Where've you been the whole night?" I'd noticed Kaitlin had taken up my approach and clutched a half-full water bottle with the cap secured.

She waved her hand around indicating a couple of different groups. "Oh, you know, just catching up with people." There was a beat of silence between the both of us as we looked upon the group. Part of it all, yet somehow not. "It's different now, isn't it?" she finally asked.

"Yeah, it is. Being the life of the party doesn't seem as interesting, or as important, as it once was."

She nodded, her eyes still fixed on everything and nothing in front of us. She mumbled something under her breath.

"What was that?"

She shook her head, clearing her thoughts. "Oh, nothing. I just said 'in the world, but not of it.' Something I've been thinking about lately."

I'd heard that before. Read it for myself. I knew what she was talking about, and it perfectly described our situation at that moment.

"I know what you mean."

She turned her head to me and smiled. A genuine smile of friendship. And so I did what any good friend-brother would do . . . snaked my arm around her neck, pulled her into my side, fisted my hand and ran it back and forth on her head messing her hair up even further.

"Argh, you are so annoying sometimes." She said it with a laugh in her voice—so I knew she wasn't really mad at me—and wriggled from my grasp. "Do you realize that?"

"I am very aware," I answered solemnly, "I'm lucky to have a friend like you."

"Yes, you are." She crossed her arms over her chest in what was supposed to be a disgruntled pose, but she had a horrible poker face.

The party had been going on long enough that people were finally beginning to ignore me. I breathed a sigh of relief. This just wasn't my scene anymore.

"So, Mr. Deep Thinker," Kaitlin started.

I pointed a finger at my chest. "Me? Deep? Never."

One side of her lips curled up in a smirk, "You can't fool me, Logan. I know there's more to you than your pretty face."

"Do not let anyone hear you say that," I said swiftly glancing around in mock frustration to see if anyone had heard, "I have a rep to uphold."

Her laugh was loud, but so were the festivities around us, so no one turned to look. "Oh yeah, I can tell that you're really concerned with upholding your old rep." She nodded down at the water in my hand.

"What can I say? I've turned over a new leaf."

"Which is exactly what I want to talk about. So, tell me what's really been going on these last few months?"

I turned weary eyes to her. There had been a lot of ups and downs during that time. Definitely decisions I wasn't proud of, but also some stuff I needed to talk to someone about.

Kaitlin's face was filled with anticipation. As if she'd been waiting to have this conversation for a while now. And in hindsight, I could see that she had.

"There was a man," I began, "and his sacrifice for all of us is what made all the difference."

———

Time flew by, and by some miracle, Kaitlin and I weren't interrupted. We'd talked about everything. I told her all about what my time as a pro-surfer had really been like.

All the details, leaving very little out.

I had expected her to look at me, eyes full of condemnation, but that never happened. Kaitlin had too big of a heart for that.

She shared about the changes happening in her life too, and

when they had really started, which was far before she'd ever mentioned anything to me.

We were so engrossed in our own conversation that we didn't realize the party had died down and we were some of the only people left. By the time we had noticed, Kaitlin thought to check her phone.

"You've got to be kidding me."

"What?" I asked.

"Ugh, Jessie. She left me here to go 'hang out' with Ryan." Kaitlin used her fingers to mark the quotes around 'hang out'. I didn't need an explanation of what that meant. "She said she's had too much to drink and let him take her home. How annoying. If she'd just left her keys with me I could have driven her car home."

Stuff like that happened all the time, but I could still understand Kaitlin's frustration. In fact, who knows if *my* ride was even still here? Time to go look around I guess.

"Come on, let's go see if Reeve ditched us, too."

We walked around for a few minutes before we found him quite literally tangled up with Rachel. I tilted my head to the side as I watched the show, feeling a little bit like a creeper for staring, but his tongue had to be halfway down her throat and it was like a train-wreck—I couldn't look away. That was some serious skill right there, just not the type you wanted to actually have.

"Logan," Kaitlin swatted my arm, "break them up or something."

I gestured towards the sand-covered couple. "I'm not breaking that up. I'm even sorry we went looking for him. That right there, is something I can never un-see."

Kaitlin huffed her irritation and then walked up to the couple and kicked Reeve's shoe. It didn't deter him from his current course of action, which I'm pretty sure was a hybrid between CPR and making-out. Kaitlin kicked the bottom of his sandal one last time with similar non-results.

Apparently fed up with the spectacle, she reached down and grabbed a handful of sand and chucked it at them and then yelled, "Hey, dork, gimme your keys so we can get home."

I laughed out loud at Reeve's shocked face when he came up for air. It bellowed out of me in waves. What tempered my amusement was Rachel's look of mortification when she realized both Kaitlin and I had been privy to her. . . ah . . . moment with him. For her sake, I forced myself back under control.

"Did you just throw sand on us?" Reeve brushed some of the granules off his shirt, but whether it was from Kaitlin tossing it on them, or them rolling around in it, who really knew.

"Yep, sure did. Now hand over your keys, lover boy. Logan and I want to head home. And we all know with his ugly face he needs all the beauty sleep he can get." She threw a smile over her shoulder at me, as if to say, 'Did you hear what I just said about you?' Guess she didn't get the memo that guys aren't as sensitive about their looks as girls.

"Yeah, that's right," I chimed in and took the wind out of Kaitlin's sails, "I need a lot of beauty rest. So, let me have them. You can come pick your car up at my place tomorrow."

"No way, man. That's my baby. No one drives her but me."

This was getting annoying. "Come on, dude. We live down the street from each other. You can walk over to pick it up in the morning."

He got to his feet. His hands and jaw clenched. It was obvious he was annoyed, but I wasn't sure if it was from us insisting we drive his new *baby*, or having interrupted his time with Rachel. I was too tired to care.

"I said no one drives her but me." Well, I guess that answered that question. He was definitely more concerned about his car than the girl he was with. I just hoped Rachel saw his behavior for what it was and used it as an excuse to leave his sorry butt behind.

"Hey, why don't you drop them off and then you and I can head somewhere together?" she suggested.

I ran a hand down my face. Nope. Lesson not learned.

He finally glanced at Rachel. "Well, yeah, I guess I can do that," he pointed a finger back at me, "but I'm just driving to your house and then you can drop her off yourself." I assumed he was talking about Kaitlin.

"Yeah, man, whatever. Let's go." At this point I just wanted to be off this beach. Kaitlin and I led the way to Reeve's car.

"Do you think he's been drinking?" she whispered in my ear.

I glanced over my shoulder. His steps were straight. Now and then he veered off the path, but it seemed to be from Rachel tugging on his arm. She was the only one of us who appeared to be tipsy, but it wasn't worth the risk. If I had to, I could call someone else to come and get us.

"Hey, man, you been drinking at all tonight?" I asked when we reached his car.

Reeve scoffed at me and opened his door. "You guys get the back."

I eyed the small backseat. Could I even fit in there? "Are you being serious, right now? There's no way my legs are gonna fit back there."

"Get in or don't, I don't care. But my girl gets the front seat." Rachel smiled widely at his words. Too bad she didn't know they were less for her benefit and more to express his irritation with me.

I grabbed the handle and jerked open the door, then moved the seat so Kaitlin and I could crawl in the back.

"I'll go in first," Kaitlin said, "Rachel can at least pull her seat up a bit to give you some more leg room," she added with a pointed glance at Rachel, who was looking everywhere but at us.

I nodded my thanks. Kaitlin crawled across the first seat and then wiggled her way into the tiny back seat, just barely squeezing her legs in between the driver's chair and her own. She winced once with the effort. It was obvious her shins and calves were being pinched.

"Reeve, come on, at least give her a few extra inches."

Without looking my way, he grunted and moved his seat up a fraction. Well, at least that was something. Kaitlin's legs were trapped for sure, but at least her circulation wasn't going to be cut off. I climbed in next and settled into the remaining tight spot. My shoulder was smashed against Kaitlin and I had to tilt my body at a weird angle to make my lower body fit. Maybe I should have called for a ride instead.

At least it was a short drive.

After adjusting the seat back and giving me a few extra inches —thank you, Rachel—she jumped into the passenger seat and bounced with excitement.

"I love your new car. I can't wait to see what it can really do," she purred suggestively in Reeve's ear. I pressed my fingers to my eyes and pushed down until I saw spots.

Real classy, Rachel.

I gritted my teeth as I waited for Reeve to start his stupid car.

That turned out to only be the start of the 'Reeve and Rachel' show. For the next ten minutes Kaitlin and I sat in uncomfortable silence as Rachel did everything except unbuckle and climb into Reeve's lap to get his attention.

Rubbing the heels of my hands down my face, I tried my best

to ignore the noises from upfront. At one point, I looked over at Kaitlin, who was red in the face, but not from embarrassment. She was trying really hard not to laugh. With every added mile we drove, Rachel's antics kicked up a notch.

Seeing Kaitlin's tightly-pressed lips and bugged eyes almost made me lose it. Especially when I caught Rachel lick the side of Reeve's face. He made a move to jerk his head away, but remembering he had an audience in the backseat he caught himself and stayed still, making some bogus comment about how sexy that was.

Big mistake, bro.

She did it again and the car veered into the oncoming lane for a moment before he forced it back.

"Okay guys, why don't you cool it while we're driving," I spoke up. "We get the point."

Wrong thing to say.

Reeve white-knuckled the steering wheel. "You got a problem with my driving, man?"

I heaved an annoyed sigh. "At the moment, yeah, I do. So, if you could just keep your focus on the road for a couple more miles, you can drive this thing however you want once you drop Kaitlin and me off."

What was his problem tonight?

It dawned on me slowly. When I would look back at this moment, I would ask myself time and time again how I couldn't have seen it sooner. Reeve only ever turned into a real jerk like this when he'd had too much to drink. I should have done more than just check his steps and take his word for it.

"I can drive this car however I want. Who are you to tell me how to drive anyway? You spend more time in the water than you do on the roads." Reeve yelled at me, and even Rachel—in her impaired state—looked a bit shocked.

Kaitlin's nails bit into the flesh on my forearm as Reeve sped the car up, swerving around corners at unsafe speeds. This portion of the road wasn't lit, so only his headlights guided him around each new bend.

Time for a new tactic.

"Yeah man, you're right. This is a pretty sweet ride. I'm sure you can really open her up on the straightaways. Why don't you slow it down, though?"

Once we got to my house I would somehow get the keys to make sure he couldn't endanger himself or Rachel further.

"You want to see her really open up?"

"No!" Kaitlin yelled.

But it was too late.

Reeve had turned his head slightly to glance at me in the backseat just as the hairpin turn appeared. Even Kaitlin's warning cry didn't give him enough time to make the proper steering corrections to keep us on the road.

Rachel screamed.

We hit the guardrail at an angle on the passenger's side of the car. My head whiplashed and smashed into the side window.

The next few moments—the last of my life— blurred into a maelstrom of noise and sensation. My life didn't flash before my eyes, but bits of glass and steel did as the vehicle tumbled on its descent.

There was a small part of my brain that knew this was very bad; people didn't just walk away from an accident like this.

Between the head injury, the chaos of the accident, and the constant tornado of bodies and debris, I could only discern the crunching of the metal around us, the screams of the people in the car, and the pain that wracked my body.

This shouldn't be the end. I didn't have enough time.

The thoughts whispered through my mind just as the motion

of the car came to a jarring stop. My head once again slammed into something hard, my vision winked in and out until it was no more.

———

Author Commentary: Chapter 4
JulieHallAuthor.com/logan-4

CHAPTER 5

I was dead.

What other reason could there be for waking up in a field of multicolored flowers? I lay on my back with my arms stretched out on either side of me, blinking against the brightness of the sky and the rainbow sprinkled greenery around me. I closed my eyes, squeezing them tight to push through the memory block I seemed to be having, and snippets of a car accident filtered through.

"Well sh—"

"Hi, there."

I jackknifed to a sitting position and turned to my left. A man —probably somewhere in his thirties with tanned skin and facial hair—sat beside me.

"Whoa, where did you come from?"

He smiled and faint laugh lines appeared around his eyes. "You wouldn't believe me right now if I told you."

"Try me," I challenged.

He shrugged. "Okay, I've always been here."

"You're right, I don't believe you."

"Told ya."

"So, I'm dead, huh?"

He just shrugged again. Not a full answer, but I guess my question had been rhetorical anyway.

"All right then, what's next?" Why prolong the inevitable?

The man beside me chuckled. "You're going to fit in here just fine, Logan."

Logan, right, that was my name. How the heck did I forget my own name? In fact, there was lots of other stuff I couldn't remember.

"Why are my memories all jumbled, right now?"

"To better adjust, everyone's memories come back at their own pace, but don't worry, you'll get them back pretty quickly."

My gut told me to trust this dude, and at the moment, I was inclined to listen to it. Not that I had much choice.

I scrubbed a hand over my face. A gesture that felt familiar to me.

"Come on, Logan," the man stood and offered me a hand up, "let's get you to orientation."

I grasped his hand and was yanked to my feet. "You have to go to orientation after you die?" That was weird.

"You're in for a lot of surprises."

———

"I don't care how long I have to stand here, I'm not moving until you tell me what happened to my friend. Do you need me to spell her name out for you again?"

The blonde angel behind the intricately-carved mahogany desk looked around nervously, obviously flustered by my behavior. I'd just been assigned the job of something called a 'hunter' and was supposed to head to their training facility to meet my mentor.

But I couldn't have cared less about that right now. I wanted to know what had happened to my friend and would wait as long as it took to get answers.

That's right, I remembered Kaitlin. In fact, I'm pretty sure I remembered everything about my life on Earth. But there was no way for me to really be sure because the irony was you never would know if there was something you'd forgotten.

"Sir—"

"Logan."

"Right, Logan. You attended orientation, so you understand how things work here," she drawled out in a sweet, southern accent. Sure, put a southern belle at the front desk so we can't get frustrated without feeling bad.

I'd been hooked up to their Matrix-like machine—the information-download minus the large insertion of needles—and received the biggest brain dump ever. Apparently, I now knew all there was to know about this realm.

I had knowledge about materializing and dematerializing objects, knew where all the main buildings were in this city, learned there were different parts of the realm, that we could feel each other's emotions through a simple brushing of skin—creepy —and even that I needed to keep my lips to myself unless I wanted a soul mate for the rest of eternity.

No, thank you.

I can do without that for a few hundred years or so, because now I had all the time in the world. I was going to live . . . er . . . um, well, be like this for the rest of eternity. No need to worry about settling down anytime soon.

So yes, I got where this lady was coming from, and even knew from the faint glow she let off that she was some type of angel, but Kaitlin had been in that car with me and I needed to know if she'd made it or not. And by 'made-it' I meant made it out alive, not made it to where I was now.

There was a soft click that came from behind the blonde angel, and then a panel opened up from what I previously had assumed to be a flat wall.

Out walked another faintly glowing angel. This one had her jet-black hair pulled into a bun and wore a severe expression to match her businesslike attire.

I'll bet she was a barrel of laughs.

I refused to be intimidated.

"I've got this, Celeste," she said as she laid a hand on the blonde's shoulder.

"Oh, phew, thanks Shannon. I'll just pop out for a minute so you guys can get this sorted."

Shannon, the new angel, nodded and waited for Celeste to leave before turning her attention to me.

"What can I help you with?" she asked calmly.

I gritted my teeth. As if she didn't already know.

"I want to know what happened to my friend, Kaitlin, who was in the same car accident as me."

"She's in this realm as well."

My heart both sank and lifted with the news. It meant that she had died, but it also meant I wasn't here alone. "I want to see her."

"You cannot."

"What?" I stiffened, stepping back sharply. Blood rushed to my head and I ground my teeth together harder than before. My jaw started to ache. "Why not?"

"For several reasons actually, but the two most pertinent to your situation being that she's been assigned to a different part of the realm—"

"Why would you do that?" My hands clenched with the desire to punch my fists through the plain white wall.

"And because she doesn't have her memories back like you do."

Well, that made a little more sense. Shannon and I stared each other down. Slowly a softer emotion leaked into her gaze.

"Logan, when she regains her memories, you'll be able to visit her. But she needs a little more time than you did. Can you give that to her?"

I sighed heavily. When it was put that way, how could I say no? The fight leaked from my body and soul. I pinched the bridge of my nose.

"How will I know when she remembers everything again?"

"I'm sure she'll reach out to you when she does."

That would have to be okay for now.

"Alright. How about Rachel and Reeve? Are they floating around up here somewhere as well?"

Shannon's lips pressed together, forming a harsh line before she spoke. "No."

"You mean they're still down on Earth walking around, living out the rest of their lives while Kaitlin and I paid for their stupidity?"

There were a few beats of silence before Shannon answered. She squinted and her upper lip curled before her features smoothed out. "I wouldn't exactly say that was the case. Reeve is currently a quadriplegic. That means that there are lots of things he will most likely never again do independently. Some of those things include getting dressed, feeding himself, using the bathroom, getting into bed, driving a—"

"Stop!" I lifted a hand to halt her flow of words, "I get what you're saying." Shannon had rattled off that list in a monotone voice that might have seemed uncaring, but I got her point. Reeve was paying dearly for his mistake.

I shoved a hand in my hair and fisted it. Bile churned and boiled in my gut.

Yeah, I was mad at him for the accident, but I didn't want him to suffer like that for the rest of his life.

I stared at the blank wall to the right of Shannon before asking my next question. "What about Rachel?"

"Rachel is physically fine. She escaped the crash with some broken bones and cuts, but nothing life threatening or permanent," I almost breathed a sigh of relief, but it would have been too soon. Shannon continued, "Except mentally she has to live the rest of her life as the only one who walked away from that accident. Many people in her situation struggle with survivor's guilt, which can manifest itself as severe anxiety, depression, social withdrawal, insomnia, night terrors, mood swings and posttraumatic stress disorder."

I couldn't see myself, but I knew the blood had drained from my face. No longer satisfied with residing in my stomach, the acidic taste of bile crawled its way up my throat.

Shannon continued, "Only time will tell how this event shapes her future. I think it's safe to say that no one escaped that crash unscathed." The last sentence was a censure to me.

I looked the angel in the eye and nodded, "Yeah, I believe you're right."

"Any more questions, or can we move on now?"

Swallowing once, I shook my head and stared at nothing. My thoughts were on the two people suffering on Earth and the one here that I wasn't allowed to contact.

I startled when she laid a hand on my shoulder. Shannon waited until I met her gaze to speak. Her eyes weren't harsh, but they spoke of a core of steel.

"Are you ready to start the first day of the rest of your existence?"

I arched a brow at her and a small barely-there smile touched her lips. Was anyone ever really ready for that?

———

I was a natural. I wasn't being prideful, it was just the simple truth. I picked up fighting skills quickly and efficiently. I'm sure being an athlete on Earth hadn't hurt either as my body quickly adjusted to the new routine of the afterlife. I knew I was a good surfer, but this was really what I was built for. I couldn't wait to go up against my first demon. The thought of protecting the living against evil didn't leave me cowering in fear, but rather got my adrenaline flowing and heart pumping.

Through hard work and practice, every weapon I touched eventually became an extension of myself. I wielded them all fluidly, gracefully, and with deadly precision.

I spent extra time in the gym simply because I wanted to, not because I had to. When I was there everything else melted into the background. And it stopped me from thinking about what I'd left behind on Earth.

And there was a hefty list of things I sometimes found myself obsessing over. My surfing career was one of the things I'd had to come to terms with losing, but it wasn't the most difficult by far. The hardest part was letting go of my parents and friends. I'd built surfing up as a big part of my identity while alive, but I now realized I should have spent more of my energy on the people that mattered instead.

It was a mistake I wouldn't get the opportunity to atone for. And that was hard. Finding meaning in my new job—what I was literally created to do—made it better. Yet even now, I had to hold myself in check. If I weren't careful I would put being a hunter at the center of my universe, exactly as I had done with surfing on Earth.

I wouldn't let this job consume me. I'd gone down that road already and knew my identity was rooted in something much more powerful than that.

After only a matter of weeks, my mentor Stephen, a former knight during the Crusades, was already talking about sending me to the gauntlet—the trials every trainee had to pass before becoming an active hunter. After passing the gauntlet, I would not only become an active hunter, but eventually a mentor myself. I truly looked forward to the challenge.

Kaitlin had visited me for a few days the previous week before returning to her part of the realm. It had been a bitter-sweet reunion between the two of us. There was sadness about everything she'd left behind, but training to be a hunter—her assigned occupation as well—came almost as natural to her as it did to me. Having a true purpose revived part of her soul.

She was also something of a novelty being one of the few female hunters. There were all types of hunters, but the vast majority of them looked like professional body builders.

Looks could be deceiving though. I'd learned that the hard way by underestimating a fellow hunter, a girl named Romona, during a sparring session Stephen had arranged. The dark-haired beauty might have appeared fragile, but she moved like the wind and packed a mean punch.

I'd learned about more than just fighting techniques the last several weeks. I'd made some interesting discoveries about my new home as well. I lived on the outskirts of a sparkling city nestled against a magnificent mountain range and giant forests. But the area I now considered home wasn't the only part of this realm.

The topography where Kaitlin resided differed from my slice of heaven. She was in a part of the realm more suited to the California girl I believed she would always be at heart. Her training center was steps from a beach, with warm light-filled days, ocean breezes, and laid-back evenings. Everything she said about it reminded me of where we'd grown up.

She tried to convince me to transfer to her part of the realm—something I'd learned was possible—but this was where I needed to be. Maybe I didn't want to be there because it was too much like my old life. Maybe it was for some other reason. I couldn't quite nail down my own hesitation.

Perhaps someday I'd go back to what I'd always known, but for now I listened to my gut and stayed put. There was a reason I'd been assigned to this part of the realm and I was curious to see what it was.

"Yo, Logan, stop showing the rest of us up," a voice boomed from the entrance of my training gym. My mentor had long since left, and I recognized the deep timbre of Alrik's voice, the mountain of a man who never seemed to take anything seriously.

"Is it *my* fault you can't keep up with this awesomeness?" I taunted back still striking the punching bag in front of me.

"Oh, young Skywalker, you have much to learn."

I grabbed the bag to stop it from swinging and shot Alrik a look. "How in the world do you know lines from *Star Wars*, old man?"

"Old man? *Old man?* That, my young friend, is a wounding blow. We both know I don't look a day over 600."

In reality, Alrik appeared to be in his late twenties. But here, where people rarely aged, it was impossible to guess anyone's true age. He claimed to be a Viking, but something about the chuckle he couldn't contain every time he mentioned it had me wondering if it was true—either way, he did play the part to perfection. With his large stature, blond hair and beard, he also happened to resemble Thor a bit too much.

"Come on, call it quits for the day. We're hitting the town tonight. Go get your smelly self cleaned up. I don't want you scaring off any of the ladies with your foul stench."

I gave myself a sniff. He wasn't wrong about my needing a shower.

"Hitting the town, huh?"

"Yes. You know. Go out with a group of your friends and do normal people things together. You did used to have a life, right?"

"Funny."

His grin widened. "Why yes, that I am."

"Humble, too," I added with mirth.

"Whoa, there. Let's not get ahead of ourselves. That's something I've never claimed to be."

I pointed a wrapped hand in his direction. "And I'll bet it's something you've never been accused of before, either."

"That is also true." He puffed out his chest as if extremely proud of that fact. I laughed off his antics.

"Where are we meeting?"

"Well, I'd say your place, but you live like a hermit out there in that cottage."

"Hey, now. It's a manly cabin and we both know it," I answered him.

He lifted his brows and hands. "If you say so. But in light of your hermit-like abode, we're gonna meet up at Kevin's place."

"The big glass building that looks like an open book, right?"

"Yep, that's the one," he backed out of the room, "We're leaving in an hour with or without you. So, you'd better get moving if you want to have time to perfectly style that head of yours."

He let the door bang shut behind him before I could defend

my grooming habits. Alrik was always giving me a hard time about my hair. He was convinced I spent hours in front of a mirror styling it, when in reality I just showered, towel-dried it, and let it fall where it wanted.

Unwrapping my hands, I threw everything in my gym bag and spent a few minutes tidying up the gym before leaving the training center.

I skipped the locker rooms in favor of showering in my cabin instead. Maybe Alrik was right. I did kind of live like a hermit out by the edge of the forest. There wasn't a path that led to my house, so I'd made a crude one with a borrowed sword from the training center. I had to hike through part of the giant redwood forest to get home. Most people lived in the populated, bustling city, but this place fit me better.

I cleared the tree line and made my way to the front of my rustic and incredibly manly cabin. It sat just within the shadows of the giant trees overlooking fields of flowers. The same one, in fact, I'd first woken up in when I'd arrived in this realm.

From the outside, it didn't appear to be anything other than a small hunting cabin, but the inside . . . well that was a different story altogether. I guess every detail hadn't simply been downloaded during orientation . . . just the highlights. Because what we could do with our living spaces was almost beyond my imagination.

I opened the front door and stepped into my beach bungalow. What one could do with a simple thought in this realm was also beyond belief. When I'd first arrived and was assigned this home to live in, I'd been less than impressed with its Spartan appearance. It had been a couple of days before I'd remembered I could change my living space into anything I desired.

Decorating wasn't really my thing, but at one point I had wanted to go to school to be an architect, and at the end of all my experimenting the inside of the cabin looked a lot like a two-story beach-themed bungalow. Smaller than the house I'd grown up in or those of my friends, but more fit to my personality.

No extra frills, mostly just the necessities, except for the sweet master bathroom I'd thought up. The shower alone was worth waiting the extra fifteen-minute walk to clean up.

If Alrik wanted to tease me about something, it should have been the exorbitant amount of time I spent in there.

My body relaxed as the spray from multiple showerheads pounded out the knots in my sore muscles.

Ah, now this is heaven.

———

Author Commentary: Chapter 5
JulieHallAuthor.com/logan-5

CHAPTER 6

*S*weat dripped down my brow, and it wasn't because of the heat. My first trip back to Earth was also my first assignment. I was more nervous than I was willing to admit, but my body's response to the unknown was giving me away.

I accompanied a small group of hunters tasked with clearing an intersection of a few demons. They were messing with the streetlights and had caused a few head-on collisions, but no deaths.

We'd been sent down to take care of the problem. Which meant killing the creatures responsible. They were lower-level demons, so it wasn't a high-risk mission, but it was still my first.

Romona was team lead on this one, and that surprised me. Not because she was a girl, but because Alrik was with us as well and I'd thought for sure he would pull seniority over her. From what I'd gathered, she'd been a hunter for a relatively short amount of time—meaning less than a decade—compared to some of the others with us.

But the team leads for each mission were chosen for more

than just the number of years they'd been a hunter. They were chosen based on their individual skills and talents, and the amount of focus they put into their missions.

I respected and appreciated that.

I glanced at my giant friend, Alrik. He'd never complained about it, but I did wonder what he thought of that way of doing things. If he truly was as old as he claimed to be, he'd be the senior ranking officer on this mission. From what I could see of his helmet-covered head, he was the picture of concentration. Exactly what I should be doing at the moment.

Snap out of it idiot!

The six of us moved forward together as a unit. I'd practiced enough times in the form-fitting body armor to be used to the weight and feel of it. Formless until we put it on, the tactical wear for hunters had hardened plates protecting our vital parts and was almost impossible to penetrate. An absolute must when fighting demons because their appendages were often sharp or serrated, not to mention their teeth which had evolved to bite into a hunter's flesh.

I'd been warned against ever letting my guard down against a demon. Demons gained their strength by feeding on negative human emotions. It was vital to their existence and part of what drove them to do the things they did. Hunters were somewhat of an addictive drug to them. We weren't necessary for their survival, but from what I'd been told we were a favorite tasty treat of theirs. If feeding off of human's negative emotions was their sustenance, then hunters were the dessert they would forgo their main course to consume.

Of course, generally speaking, they hated humans regardless. Thinking themselves the more superior beings, every demon had once been an angel who'd fought against the Creator, and had ultimately been cast out of His perfect realm. They'd been condemned to live out their existence on Earth, or worse, the realm beneath. So, their manipulations against the human race went deeper than mere survival; they enjoyed the pain, chaos and destruction they caused.

I shook my head to get it back in the game. The helmet I wore weighed my head down and restricted some of my view. It was the one part of the armor that took a little getting used to. I wished we didn't need them, but since we could still be knocked out, it was a necessary evil.

It felt very strange to be creeping around at night in the suburban areas knowing that no one except other hunters or demons could actually see us. After being in another realm for the last several months, being back on Earth was odd. Like discovering I'd spent a lifetime colorblind, but never realized until I was healed. Earth now seemed dull in comparison to the brilliance of my new home.

The streets we walked down looked nothing like where I'd grown up, which I appreciated. We were in the middle of America, far away from the ocean. That helped me concentrate so memories of my home, family, and friends wouldn't cloud my judgment.

Romona held up a fist signaling we should all stop. Being toward the rear of the line of hunters, I wasn't sure what lay ahead. She motioned for us to draw our weapons, which meant that she'd spotted the demons we'd come to slaughter.

I drew in a steadying breath. This was it; this was the moment I'd been incessantly training and waiting for.

I stayed light on the balls of my feet. Romona turned to the group and held up two fingers, indicating there were two demons. With a few more hand gestures she let us know we were splitting into two groups and attacking all at once. Romona, Alrik and I in a group, and Jason, Kevin and my mentor, Stephen in the other.

Stephen was being reassigned to another part of the realm on request, so this would be our first and last mission together. He gave me a wide grin before slipping away with the other hunters to attack from a different angle.

"You sure you're ready for this?" ribbed Alrik. I pressed my lips together and nodded once. Now wasn't the time for a chat.

"Okay then, you just yell if you need some saving. Damsels in distress are my specialty."

Romona glanced back and rolled her eyes at us before shaking her head.

"They're in position," she whispered. She was peering around the side of a building, so she alone knew what was going on. "We're going in three . . . two . . . one." And she took off sprinting into the street.

Dang, the girl could run fast!

Alrik and I caught up to her just as she reached the intersection and jumped straight into the air. I wasn't expecting that move. And where were the demons?

The shriek that rent the air could only be described as ungodly.

I gritted my teeth and almost dropped my sword to cover my ears.

It wasn't just the volume of the noise that was awful, but the pitch was high enough to make you drop to your knees. Stephen had warned me about it, but even his explanations didn't come close to the real thing.

Something fell from the sky with a thud that shook the ground.

Romona stood on the creature's chest, breathing hard with her sword positioned at its unprotected . . . ah, stomach . . . I think.

So that's where she'd been.

I checked my surroundings and sure enough another demon was up on a pole across the intersection and the second group of hunters was fighting to bring it down.

Man, demons were ugly.

Blackened scale-like skin stretched unnaturally over its flesh. Formerly angels, the demons' bodies had transformed to mirror the evil that lurked in their hearts. Since all their goodness had been twisted and warped into something evil, their bodies were twisted and warped as well.

This fella must have been extra evil because it looked like he'd fallen out of the ugly tree and hit every branch on the way down . . . and then some.

One of his limbs stuck out of his midsection and he used it to swat at Romona, who was trying to hack it off with her sword.

Most of their skin was extremely hard, like armor, which was unfortunate when trying to figure out where to stab to pack the most punch. Demons had a few vulnerable parts, usually around the joints, but they were difficult to locate and even harder to reach.

The thing didn't have a neck, but rather a head that attached directly to its upper body. We were trained to go for the neck first—if it had one—because that's one of their most vulnerable places.

Decapitation was a very successful way to vanquish a creature of any kind.

This monster reeked of sulfur, and the scent burned my nostrils.

This demon-fighting business was going to take some getting used to.

"Anytime now, guys!" Romona roared.

Right.

I'd been gawking at my first view of a demon rather than helping her fight.

Rookie mistake.

I don't know what Alrik's excuse was.

I jumped into action. Plunging my blade forward, I expected the tip to sink into the being's side.

I'd put a lot of force behind my attack, but was thrown off balance when it skidded across the side of the demon's armor-like hide, giving off a piercing metal-on-metal sound.

My training finally kicked in and I scanned the demon for weak points. Spots on its body where the flesh was slightly different meant we could pierce it with our weapons.

There, just under the appendage protruding from its midsection the blackened scales were missing and there was a section of penetrable flesh.

The creature threw Romona from its body and struggled to its . . . er . . . feet? Less like feet, more like stumps with jagged looking claws.

Alrik took the opportunity to attack from behind, swiping with his massive sword. The demon let out another ear-splitting cry, and swung around to its new threat. Alrik had cleaved a nice chunk of flesh from its back, but it wasn't enough to slay the creature.

Time to get back in the fight.

I aimed for the spot Alrik had already opened and my blade sunk a few inches into the unprotected flesh. One second, I was getting ready to push my weapon fully into the demon, and the next I was flying through the air.

My face throbbed and the sky above spun. I blinked until my vision cleared and was forced to sit up as my mouth filled with blood.

I spat on the ground and along with the unsavory bloody mix was a chunk of something familiar.

I ran my tongue along the top row of my teeth and sure enough, I was missing one of the front ones. I looked down to see it lying on the asphalt beside me.

Just great. I'm never going to live this one down.

"Logan! Break time is over, man. Time to help us finish Big Ugly off."

I sprang to my feet. I'd worry about the tooth later.

"Keep it distracted," I yelled to Romona and Alrik, "I see one of its weak points and I'm going to try to reach it."

Without questioning me, my fellow hunters obeyed my command and both moved in to attack together, purposefully keeping its attention on them, even though none of their blows would leave more than a scratch on the creature.

They trusted I had a plan. And I did.

While Romona and Alrik played a game of swing-and-duck with the demon, I moved around its side, and just as it lifted that weird arm-like thing coming out of its stomach, I used all my strength to thrust my sword into the base of where the limb met its body, and forced the blade into its innards.

The guttural cries of the dying demon were loud enough to make me wish I'd figured out a way to lop its head off instead.

It flailed and tried in vain to pull out the sword that I'd left in its gut. But the thrashing proved futile. My weapon was lodged at just the right spot that it couldn't be reached.

Without my sword, I backpedaled a safe distance from the raging creature. Romona and Alrik used that as an opportunity to hack off its middle appendage and sink their own weapons into its guts.

Black blood shot out of the wound and sprayed Alrik, who wiped his face with the back of his arm. Since that was also covered in the demon's goo he only managed to smear it around more.

I may have lost a tooth, but at least I wasn't covered in that foul-smelling liquid.

Romona delivered the killing blow to the demon by sinking a dagger into one of its slitted eye-sockets.

The creature crashed to the ground, and after a few moments dissolved into ash and shadow.

Our weapons, although still covered in black ichor, lay unharmed. I bent over and retrieved my sword, wiped it on a nearby bush and slid it back into the scabbard.

Whoops and howls came from the other group, who had dispatched their demon first and apparently—rather than helping us—had stood back to enjoy the show. Stephen stepped forward and slapped me on the back . . . hard. I forced myself not to stumble.

"Well done, Logan. It looks like my work here is complete," he said with his thick French accent.

I smiled back at him. I was going to miss my friendly crusader.

He grimaced. "Sorry about your face, though. You're going to have a hard time getting a girl to take you someday looking like that." He shook his head. "It's too bad too, because you used to be so good-looking."

Surely they could replace my tooth. Right?

Stephen bent over and started laughing.

"Don't worry, Logan, we'll get you to the healing center and get you fixed up right away."

"Thanks," I said, hearing a lisp in my voice and rolling my eyes at the howl of laughter it brought from not only Stephen, but Alrik as well. I hoped I'd live this down one day.

———

Author Commentary: Chapter 6
JulieHallAuthor.com/logan-6

CHAPTER 7

"on't look behind you, the Harbinger of Death is headed this way," Alrik whisper-yelled in the cafeteria.

"Alrik," Kevin reprimanded, "she can probably hear you."

"I think he's counting on it," I piped in.

"Which is why I always choose not to entertain his antics," Shannon said as she stepped up to our table.

I tilted my head back so I could see her. Her hair was up in a tight bun, like always, not a single wrinkle on her business-like attire, while a very faint glow emanated from her.

Shannon often interacted with the hunters. Kind of like one of the overseers of the business-end of our operation. Many of our missions and orders came through her, although I'd put money down that she'd never been in an actual battle before. Yet, despite her somewhat-stuffy demeanor and her dislike of smiles in general, in a weird way she was growing on me.

Sure, she wasn't the cuddliest of angels, but she took her job seriously and worked hard, and I respected that.

"What can we help you with today, Shannon?" I asked with my head still tilted backwards. She frowned down on me in disapproval. My smile broadened.

"Logan, if you're finished eating I have a new trainee to introduce you to."

"Fresh meat? Oh yeah, I'm definitely in!" I jumped out of my chair, ready to meet my next mentee. I'd already trained two other hunters, so I held a certain amount of confidence now about my assignments. "See you guys later," I waved to the table as I turned to follow Shannon.

"Don't forget to bring him around later so we can place our bets," Alrik bellowed when I was on the other side of the busy room.

I winced when Shannon came to a sudden stop.

Thanks, Alrik.

I glanced over my shoulder and he was doubled over, laughing at the predicament he'd purposefully put me in.

Shannon did a slow turn to face me.

"Tell me you all aren't still mistreating our new hunters."

I held my hands up in front of me; a look of pure innocence sculpted my face, "Mistreating? Noooooo. No one is doing that."

"Hazing is not allowed."

"I can promise you, Shannon, we are not hazing the new hunters." Nope. We were just taking bets on how long they'd last on their first day before puking their guts out. In fact, it was kind of a bonding experience since it had happened to all of us. I grinned broadly at Shannon when she lifted one brow at me.

"You'd better not be. I expect more from you, Logan."

I cleared my throat and nodded once. I couldn't help but feel like a scolded child. Alrik was probably dying of laughter right now.

"So, the new guy?" I prompted to keep us on track.

"Right. His name is Morgan. Let's go so I can introduce you two and you can get started." Back to business. At least she was predictable.

When we walked into the training gym a few minutes later, someone was wailing on the punching bag. His dark mop of black hair was slicked to his forehead with sweat. I immediately went into mentor mode and began to assess his stance and movements.

I was somewhat impressed.

"Morgan," Shannon raised her voice to be heard over his fists smashing into the bag.

The guy stopped his jabs and turned his head to look at us. He lifted his chin in greeting as he started unwrapping his hands. Once done he tossed them into a gym bag and made his way to us.

"Hello there, lovely Shannon. It's good to see you again so soon. Hey there, mate," his British-accented voice rang strong as he addressed me and held out his hand, "My name is Morgan. So, you're to be my task master, eh?"

I waited a beat before grasping his hand. Not because of anything he said or did, but simply because the empathy link still made me a little uneasy.

This guy was an open book. All I got from him was a laid-back vibe laced with mild curiosity.

"Hey, man. Yeah, I'm Logan," I pumped his hand in return. I glanced toward the punching bag and then back at him, "Looks like you have a little head-start over most of the new hunters."

Morgan lifted an arm and scratched the back of his head, "Yeah, I know my way around a gym."

"Morgan was on the cusp of being a professional soccer player," Shannon informed me.

"That would be football where I'm from, luv."

Shannon tipped her head in acknowledgement.

"Really?" My interest was piqued. "I was a pro-surfer for about two minutes before I died." I chuckled at the career that never was.

"Hey mate, that's terrific," he held out a fist for a bump and I knocked knuckles with him.

We were going to get along just fine.

———

I stretched a gloved hand down to help Morgan up off the ground. It had taken me a full five minutes longer than usual to best him today. Training him was almost effortless.

He picked up techniques quickly, worked hard, learned how to materialize and dematerialize objects faster than anyone I'd ever seen—myself included—and on top of that was easy going and quick to laugh.

We'd hit it off immediately and he was quickly becoming not *just* my trainee, but my friend as well.

"Good job, you," Morgan said as I helped haul him to his feet. He dematerialized his sparring helmet, which had covered his face, and I did the same. Because he was so proficient in materializing, I'd moved him to only working with weapons and armor he could create himself. His breathing was slightly elevated from exertion, but still far more controlled than either of my other trainees at this point.

"I should be saying the same to you. You made me work a little for that one."

"Oh, get off it," he shoved my shoulder good-naturedly.

My laugh was cut off by a metallic blur and then I was lying flat on the mat with the wind punched out of my lungs, staring at the ceiling rafters.

What just happened?

A weight on top of me was making it hard to breathe. A hunter, covered from head to toe in armor, except for a white-blonde pony-tail shooting out of the top of her helmet—well she'd obviously made an adjustment to the standard issue gear—was sitting on my chest. Not straddling me or even trying to hold me down. But sitting on my chest . . . with her legs crossed in front of her . . . and laughing.

I shook my head and then gave Kaitlin a good shove. She tumbled off me to the mat, but continued to laugh as I caught my breath.

"I told you I'd best you eventually, Logan."

I lumbered to my feet and pointed a finger at her, "That was cheating."

She rolled on the ground like a puppy, giggling like a maniac. "Yeah, like demons fight fair," she sat up suddenly and threw her arms in the air and yelled, "I win."

"Brat," I rolled my eyes at her antics even as I cracked a smile. Kaitlin had an infectious personality that was hard to not go along with.

Finally gaining control of herself, she rolled to a sitting position and dematerialized her armor, leaving her in typical workout clothes—tight-fitting black leggings and a yellow sports tank. She resembled a bumblebee.

"You have to admit, that was pretty good."

Before I could answer her, Morgan's deep British voice cut in, "I'm not sure if he's capable of admitting defeat, luv. It's not hard-wired into him. But anytime you want to spar with me, I'd be a willing participant. I might even concede defeat."

Watching Kaitlin's eyes widen, I coughed to cover my laugh. Morgan was a shameless flirt, but he'd just laid it on thick. My California girl was speechless. Not something that happened often.

I glanced back and forth between the two of them.

Morgan stood in full armor—except for his helmet—his arms crossed over his chest, feet spread wide, and a cocky smile on his face while he boldly ogled Kaitlin.

Kaitlin sat cross-legged on the padded mat. Leaning back on her arms she stared up at him with rounded eyes and parted lips.

The longer the silence stretched on, the greater my urge grew to slowly back out of the gym and leave the two of them alone.

This was an interesting development.

"Do you need a hand up, luv?" Morgan stretched his arm out so that his hand was within Kaitlin's reach. She did her best impression of a deer in headlights. A deep rumble of laughter finally burst from my chest. It snapped Kaitlin out of whatever trance Morgan had put her in.

Maybe it was the accent that had gotten her? Maybe it was more?

She cleared her throat and avoided eye contact with Morgan as she got to her feet—without his assistance—and immediately started playing with the end of her ponytail.

"Don't be a jerk," Kaitlin growled under her breath as my laughter subsided. Her eyes narrowed as she said it, which recharged my amusement.

"Logan, are you going to introduce me to this lovely bird of yours?"

Kaitlin turned on me, "Did he basically just call me a 'chick' and insinuate I was your possession?"

"Yes. He totally just did that," I said. Then, seeing shock on

Kaitlin's face, quickly followed with, "But, I think it's just a British thing. He didn't mean any harm by it."

"Yes," Morgan jumped in, clearly not bothered at all by Kaitlin's ire, "please excuse my coarse language, lovely friend of Logan's whose name I still don't know. I've spent entirely too much time with a bunch of rough-around-the-edges male hunters and it has obviously affected me in a most negative way. A thousand apologies." Morgan hammered it up by bowing at the waist to Kaitlin. Her brow furrowed in return.

"Is he for real?" Kaitlin asked me, jerking a thumb, but not her gaze, in his direction, "Does he talk like that all the time?"

"No, not usually. I think you're getting special treatment."

"Oh, lucky me."

"Hey, mate, what kind of wingman are you? Bad form," Morgan complained.

"Sorry man, I didn't realize my duties as a mentor also encompassed wingman."

"When a beautiful lady who isn't already spoken for is involved, it's implied."

Kaitlin cut her hand through the air, "Okay, enough with the fake charm. Logan, introduce us already so I can go back to ignoring him and spend some time with you. I have an afternoon off today and I'd planned on gracing you with my presence."

I couldn't hide the amused smile on my face as I made the introduction. "Kaitlin, this is Morgan, my new trainee. Morgan, this is Kaitlin, an old friend of mine not just from here, but Earth as well."

"Well, that hardly did me justice," Morgan grumbled.

"Nice to meet you . . . ah . . . kinda, Morgan. Now I'm planning on stealing your mentor for the rest of the day. Have a nice after-life." Kaitlin grabbed my arm and tried to haul me from the gym, which she found was a fruitless endeavor, but was entertaining to both Morgan and myself.

Kaitlin was becoming a great huntress, but I had almost a hundred pounds on her. Unless she did another sneak attack, she wasn't going to be able to make me budge unless I wanted to be moved. And messing with her was way more amusing than going along with her plan.

"Come on, you over-grown toddler," Kaitlin grunted and jerked on my arm. I took half a step in her direction.

"You know, Kaitlin, I can't leave Morgan all alone."

"What?" she dropped both my arm and her jaw.

"Yeah, he's my trainee. I have to look out for him now. He's going to have to come with us if you want to hang out." Morgan's smile broadened and Kaitlin scowled at me.

"You're joking, right?"

"'Fraid not, my dear friend. It's just the right thing to do. I can't leave poor Morgan to fend for himself when he's so new here." My straight-faced delivery testified to my ability to cloak my emotions, as inside I howled with laughter. Morgan certainly didn't need help making friends, but she didn't know that.

Kaitlin played with her ponytail as she looked back and forth between us. Morgan dropped his head forward a bit as if rejected, and gazed at Kaitlin with puppy-dog eyes.

I remained stone-faced because I knew if I moved a muscle, I would break down with laughter. I'm pretty sure Morgan was going for the see-how-pathetic-and-humble-I-am expression, but he just reminded me of a cartoon character.

"But, Logan," Kaitlin whined, "I only have an afternoon and evening to hang out. Do we really have to bring him with us?"

"Standing right here, listening to every word you say, luv."

Kaitlin shot him a withering look. "I don't know," she said to me, her voice lowering slightly, "you know I don't trust guys with beards and accents."

"Since when?"

"Since now."

"Hey, this isn't a beard. Just a bit of scruff. I can shave it off if that's what you'd prefer." Morgan chimed in.

Kaitlin rolled her eyes. "Fine. He can tag along," she pointed a finger at Morgan, "But just so you know, I'm going to pretend you aren't here."

"Oh," Morgan perked up, "a challenge. I like it," he rubbed his hands together, "Let the games begin."

"See!" Kaitlin turned on me, "That's exactly what I was worried about. Have a talk with your boy here about proper American manners. I'll meet you at the pond outside the gym when you guys have cleaned up."

"Luv, I'm British. We invented manners. Or didn't you know?" Morgan said and winked at her.

"You got it," I cheerfully answered and held my fist out for Morgan to bump without looking in his direction.

"Men," she grumbled and then stomped from the training gym, letting the door bang unnecessarily loud on her way out.

Kaitlin rarely got this flustered around guys, but somehow Morgan had quickly gotten under her skin. I'd let Morgan work out whether that was going to turn into a good or bad thing.

"Oh, I like her," Morgan said, his eyes still fixed on the gym door, "That one has spunk and spirit." There was a gleam in his eye that gave me a slight pause in my decision to force the two of them to spend time together. I liked Morgan, and wanted Kaitlin to like him, too. I wanted my friends to get along. Still, she was like a sister and I didn't want Morgan playing with her emotions.

"Man, she's basically my oldest friend and like a sister to me.

You act inappropriately towards her and I'll have to break something important. We clear?"

Morgan's eyes drifted to mine, and a smile lit his face. "Crystal, mate."

Author Commentary: Chapter 7
JulieHallAuthor.com/logan-7

CHAPTER 8

I crept along the deserted driveway, each step calculated to avoid making noise. It was late in the afternoon and the sun hung at the horizon's edge. Our rendezvous point was a mile behind us and we had about another hour to scope out the old house.

"So, you're saying she hasn't mentioned me at all?"

I shot Morgan a look that clearly said *shut up*, but he ignored me. We'd been training together for several months and Morgan was flying through the program. He'd passed the gauntlet several weeks ago and had already experienced his first few missions on Earth. He wore a sword secured at his waist, but archery was what he really excelled at. His bow was slung across his chest and a quiver full of arrows strapped to his back.

I'd never seen anyone's arrow slice the air with such accuracy. The more he trained, the faster he became at notching and aiming. When we were at the archery range, his movements blurred from his frenzied pace and then I'd look up to see he'd hit the bull's-eye on not just his own target, but the others lined up to the right and left as well. A few times a week he trained with one of our archery specialists because he'd far surpassed my skill level with that weapon.

I'd started calling him 'Katniss' every now and then just to mess with him. It was one of the few things that actually got under his skin.

We moved slowly, scouting an area of reported increased demon activity. An abandoned house some kids had used to conduct fake séances not realizing they'd attract the attention of a horde of demons instead of Casper the friendly ghost.

Morgan, however, seemed more interested in pumping me for details about Kaitlin than the mission. At first, I was amused at Kaitlin's response to Morgan—interest covered with wary suspicion. It had been entertaining to watch Morgan turn into somewhat of a performing monkey the few times Kaitlin had come to visit. Now, it was just plain annoying.

Morgan continued peppering me with questions as we crept up to the property.

"Dude," I glared at him, "Not the time, alright?"

He winced, "Yeah, sorry mate. You're right, I should be taking this more seriously. Okay boss, following your lead."

I nodded and started forward, but jerked to a stop when a shadowy figure crossed in front of the ransacked house. Morgan and I crouched low to the ground to avoid being seen. Our mission was supposed to be strictly recon. We were not there to engage any demons.

We watched the creature pass by the front of the house two more times, but didn't see any other activity.

It appeared the reports had some merit to them, but rather than a horde of demons, there was only a single one preying off the unsuspecting high-schoolers who thought they were having a night of silly fun.

"There's only one," Morgan said in a low voice a touch above a whisper, "It's not even that big. We can take it, between the two of us."

I couldn't say the thought hadn't crossed my mind as well, but dispatching the demon would be against our orders.

"That's not what we're here for."

"Yeah, I know. But it's just one. And I'm kinda itching for some real action."

I glanced back at Morgan. His face was serious and his eyes blazed. "Better to ask forgiveness than permission?"

"Easy for you to say when it's *my* neck on the line with Shannon when we come back covered in demon blood."

"Might be worth it just to see the look on her face."

I shook my head, wanting to be responsible and follow-through with our orders.

"Oh, come on Logan. Look, it's just a little one. I only see two spiked tails. You know we can easily take it out. Then, ta-da, demon issue gone. We return conquering champions, knights-in-shining-armor, blah, blah, blah. We'll be heroes, mate!"

I shook my head again. Why he and Alrik didn't get along was a mystery to me. Maybe it was because they were too similar; although, while Morgan had Alrik's humor and charm, he took hunting very seriously and trained hard. Maybe Alrik had been in the game too long and it was getting to him. Or maybe it just wasn't his personality to take anything too seriously. Either way it didn't matter. I'd accepted Alrik for who he was.

As if I couldn't tell exactly what he was doing, Morgan slowly crept forward. I could've stopped him, and probably should have. But I hadn't spilled any demonic blood in a while, and this creature appeared to be easy pickings.

I pushed down the nagging feeling in my gut and moved forward with Morgan.

"Okay, fine. But if we're doing this, we're going to do it the smart way," I whispered my plan of attack to Morgan and he nodded in understanding.

I was going to engage the creature first, and while it was distracted, Morgan would swing around and attack from behind. Strategically speaking, it was a sound and simple plan, and I had zero doubts we'd take care of the problem quickly.

Had we stumbled across one of the greater demons—who used to be warrior angels before their fall from grace—I never would have entertained the idea of a fight without at least a full unit of hunters and even perhaps a few angels, but this creature appeared to be some sort of underling. A bottom feeder in the demon hierarchy.

It even appeared to be sickly. Its dark, scaly skin was stretched tight over its distorted features. This one was somewhat humanoid in appearance and its appendages that mimicked arms and legs appeared devoid of muscle of any kind. Like flesh wrapped around bone.

How did a demon even become that emaciated?

My subconscious issued a warning, but at this point, I'd already stepped into the clearing in front of the dilapidated house and drawn attention to myself.

The shriek the demon let out upon spotting me was one of the loudest I'd ever heard. What this thing lacked in girth it made up for in noise.

Something warm trickled down the side of my neck and I wondered if the sound had ruptured one of my eardrums. No time to check, I lifted my weapon and rushed the blackened form.

I slashed my sword up at the creature a moment before its claws reached me. I aimed for its midsection, but my blow was deflected by one of its boney upper limbs. Hitting it was like striking my sword against a piece of hardened steel, making my weapon shake and the vibrations travel up my arms.

The demon swung at me again with its sharp claws and I rolled out of the way. I kept the creature busy, making sure its attention stayed on me while I waited for Morgan to sneak up behind it.

I managed to get in some superficial hits, which did minimal damage and only seemed to make it angrier. The longer we fought, the more the creature's energy flagged. It was obvious in the decreased speed of its movements and its clumsy attacks. Something else was going on here; this wasn't how demons usually behaved, but I couldn't focus on the mystery at the moment.

I'd spotted Morgan as he sprinted straight for the demon from behind. I kept it engaged and then with one powerful thrust, Morgan's blade punched through the demon's midsection. It howled again and pawed at the sword protruding from its gut, cutting itself as it tried to push the blade back out the way it had come through.

With as much strength as I possessed, I brought my own sword up and across its neck, cleaving its head right from its body. The pieces of broken demon—head and body—fell to the ground and crumbled to ash.

Morgan looked up at me with a broad smile and then retrieved his sword from the mess at our feet.

"You see mate, that's what I'm talking—"

"Down!" I shouted at Morgan, who despite being mid-sentence heeded my command. A barbed demon tail sailed through the air where Morgan's head had been a moment before.

Having trained together, we worked like a well-oiled

machine. Morgan rolled and shot to his feet, quickly taking position behind my back..

"Where did they all come from?" he asked. Whether the question was meant for me or just for himself, I wasn't sure.

"This was a trap. We're surrounded," I answered him anyway. "That first demon was the bait."

"What do we do then?"

"We fight."

———

I lost track of time as Morgan and I slashed, hacked, and fought against the onslaught of demons. They landed a few blows on us, but our armor had taken most of the beating. Morgan now fought with his left arm because the right one was most likely broken.

This was no ordinary demon ambush. I'd been a hunter for almost a year and a half and had never seen or heard of demons behaving this way. Demons were a little like sharks around hunters. It was something we often used to our advantage. They were easy to work into a frenzy in their desire to chomp down on us, and that made them sloppy and marginally easier to fight.

But this group of demons was different.

I'd witnessed demons fight and injure each other to get to a hunter first, but these ones fought as a unit, and seemed uninterested in taking us down.

They were trying to wear us out—which was working—but for what reason I didn't know. Since the fighting never ceased I didn't have a chance to think through the logic of it.

"The house!" Morgan yelled to me.

We'd found ourselves herded at the front of the abandoned

house we'd been scouting earlier. It was now fully dark, and with no electricity inside it was hard to see, but with demons around us on three sides, and an empty building at our back, there was one obvious choice of retreat.

We'd already missed our rendezvous for our transport back to the realm, but if we could somehow manage to free ourselves of this mess, we could still get home.

"Go! I'll cover you until you get the door open. I'll follow after."

Morgan didn't need any more encouragement. He lifted a foot and shoved the demon he'd been fighting off him, then sprinted for the warped door at my back.

The snap and groan of wood splintering reached my ears.

"I'm in!" he yelled a moment later.

I swung my blade in a wide arc to give myself as much room as possible to make a run for the door. Once inside, I wasn't sure what we were going to do. I just prayed there was a back entrance we could escape from that wasn't surrounded, or that a group of hunters had already been dispatched to find us since we'd missed our rendezvous window.

I dashed up the rickety steps, expecting to either feel the slash of a claw at my back or for my foot to punch through the decaying wood beneath me, but by some miracle, I actually made it into the house safely.

Slamming the door shut behind me and pressing my weight against it to stop the demons from entering, I scanned the room for Morgan.

There was a thud at my back and my whole body jarred as demons struck the door from the outside.

My eyes darted around the room, but Morgan wasn't there.

Morgan was as loyal of a person as I'd ever met, so the idea that he'd left without me only flitted through my mind. He had to be around here somewhere.

"Morgan!" I yelled as the door behind me shook violently with the force of demons' bodies being thrown against it.

"Logan, run!"

Morgan's muffled shout came from somewhere below, to the right. I jerked my head in that direction and barely made out an open doorway in the dim light. It was pitch black beyond the threshold.

Why in the world would Morgan have run into the basement when we should have been leaving the house?

The door behind me shook again, reminding me I was running out of time.

If there were living humans in the area, the demons wouldn't have been allowed to slam into the door like they were now, but seeing as we were alone in the middle of nowhere, without any witnesses, they could bring this house to the ground without repercussions.

I couldn't leave Morgan, so there really wasn't a decision to be made.

I pushed back on the door, only then noticing the deadbolt—the lock on the handle having been busted by Morgan upon entry.

Stupid, why didn't I check for another lock sooner?

I was bending under the very pressure I'd been trained to endure. I twisted the deadbolt. That wouldn't keep the demons out for long, but it might buy me a few extra moments.

I gritted my teeth and suppressed the urge to punch my hand through the wall.

How could I have been so reckless? I let this happen. This was all on me.

Shoving off the front door I sprinted for the black hole in front of me and was swallowed by the darkness.

———

Author Commentary: Chapter 8
JulieHallAuthor.com/logan-8

CHAPTER 9

I awoke to yelling. Loud agony and despair-filled shouts.

They were my own.

Blackness filled my vision and pushed its way into my being. Hatred and fury rolled in my gut in merciless never-ending waves. I was emotionally undone, physically restrained and out of my mind at the same time.

And then the agony stopped.

Had I just imagined it?

My eyes slowly adjusted to the dimly-lit room at the same rate as my mental haze dissipated. It was only when clarity returned, that I fully appreciated the horror that had befallen us.

My arms were spread wide overhead. My wrists locked in chains that were attached to some old, rusty pipes in the basement of what I assumed was the house we had entered. My shoulders ached from having my full weight on them for who knew how long. My toes brushed the floorboards, bare feet scrambling for purchase on the floor below me, only to slip in something warm and slick.

I shuddered when I realized it was my own blood, which had poured out of the gash on my shoulder.

Stripped of my body armor to the waist, the shirt underneath was shredded to rags. I tilted my head far enough to recognize the shoulder wound for what it was. Not made from the slashing of claws or weapons, but distinct bite-marks gouged deep into my flesh.

I'd been fed on. And I probably would be again soon.

A moan from the other side of the room drew my attention. I squinted, barely able to make out the figure across from me. He mirrored my position.

Morgan, from what I could tell, wasn't fairing much better than myself—worse in fact. A rope looped around my gut, like a lasso, and tightened. Dread locked in my chest and spread its icy tendrils throughout my whole body.

"Morgan," I tried to call out to him, but was hindered by the rasp in my voice. It was as if my vocal cords had been stripped from me. I moved my tongue around to build up moisture in my mouth, but it was in vain. There wasn't enough wetness to swallow and help sooth my damaged throat.

Putting every reserve of energy I had into the one action, I called out again. This time creating more volume to wield, but my words were unintelligible.

"Logan?" Morgan's voice sounded as shredded as my own.

I gulped down what little liquid had accumulated in my throat. "Yeah. Are you alright?"

Morgan made a noise that I interpreted as a humorless laugh.

"Just peachy," was his sarcastic response, "So, mate, what do the training books say about getting out of a situation like this?" It took him several tries through fits of coughing, to get the words fully out.

There was a rattling sound in his voice that concerned me. I had to remind myself that our bodies couldn't be destroyed. But right on the tail of that thought was a stark reminder of how badly we could be hurt because of it.

What had happened? How we had ended up in this pit?

"They'll send a team to locate us," I assured him, as well as myself.

Yes, this was bad. But the other hunters knew our last known location, and could find us anywhere on Earth through their tracking system. It was only a matter of time before we were rescued.

A fit of wet coughs racked Morgan's body before he spat something to the ground. Probably a wad of blood, we were both drenched in it—demons' as well as our own.

The slow creak of a door opening above us gave me a burst of hope. Thank goodness, they'd come for us quickly. But my heart plummeted and adrenaline spiked when the chirping and gurgling sounds of demon communication snaked its way to my ears.

After that the door closed and something came stomping down the steps.

A darkened mass blocked my view of Morgan.

A fire hose of flames shot out from the black mass and momentarily blinded me, forcing my lids closed. When I opened them again, an angel stood between us.

But there was no comfort in that. For this was the one angel every hunter hoped never to meet.

"I have a proposition for you." His silky voice was a clever disguise. As clever as the false skin that he now wore. For standing before Morgan and me, was the King of Hell himself. And apparently, he'd come to make a deal. But everyone knew you didn't make a deal with the devil without trading in your soul.

———

I'd lost track of time and existed in cycles of pain, broken by short reprieves. It had to have been days, yet we still hadn't been rescued.

They were searching for us though. A group of hunters had passed outside the single window that opened to the basement where we were being held. The glass was small and covered in grime—impossible to see through—but the quiet steps of my fellow hunters still penetrated my fogged mind.

I had strained to yell out to them in my broken voice, but barely a sound escaped.

At least a dozen demons scurried into the basement with us, leaving a few of their companions above to be slaughtered by the contingent of hunters sent to retrieve us.

This was it, this torture would finally end! I'd thought.

We waited and waited through the sounds of battle above us. But they never came.

Despair strangled any joy I had felt, and tears streamed down my face when I realized they were retreating—leaving Morgan and me behind in this never-ending nightmare.

Morgan remained unconscious the entire time, and there was a small mercy in that. It would have been another form of torture having come that close to freedom, only to watch it slip away.

As far as I could tell, Morgan and I were demon chow twice a day. After weeks, our bodies were riddled with scars and torn flesh. Our minds were just as broken—maybe even more so.

Demons were beings filled with everything dark and ugly in the world—they absorbed and churned in all the hate, wrath, lust, greed, jealousy, and just plain blackness out there. Whenever one of the creatures visited us, the empathy link we experienced in our realm sprang to life.

Day after day we were forced to absorb what they felt, and it was incapacitating in a way that went beyond physical pain. The demons got some sort of drug-like high in return.

The bite was necessary during battle so they remained latched to our body, but trussed up like this, they could also sink their claws into our flesh to open the link. I didn't know which method was worse.

The cycle of agony went on and on for days that never ended.

The only thing keeping us from fading into oblivion was the impossibility of doing so after death. Our immortality in the afterlife had become a curse; there was something truly worse than death, and we were experiencing it.

And then one day, the Prince of Darkness came to us again.

He sauntered down the stairs, his pace unhurried. I noticed the difference in his stomping from the claws that normally scraped against the wooden planks leading to our basement prison. A faint rustling of something brushing down the steps reached my ears. Like the sound of heavy fabric being dragged, although I doubted that was it.

When he finally came into view I recognized the noise for what it really was, large black wings—similar in size to those of the archangels—jutted up from his back. But where angel's wings had feathered layers, his looked to be made of black, membranous leather cloaked in smoke and shadow.

Devoid of any strength, Morgan and I hung listlessly from the chains wrapped around our wrists that bound us to this prison. My body was clothed in remnants alone. Rags hung from a body that had not only lost muscle mass but had stopped healing as well. Old wounds oozed what little liquid still pumped through my veins. In some ways, I had become a creature of darkness.

I hissed at the monster that was a picture of vitality where

Morgan's and my ravished bodies were little more than mostly-drained meat suits.

There was something so unbelievably grating about watching him walk around in his angel disguise, the ultimate wolf in sheep's clothing. I supposed he took on the likeness of what he once was, an angel of light.

I wanted to yell and lash out at him, but I barely had enough energy to lift my head.

He ignored us for a while, moving around the small space, adjusting various objects I could not see. Then he began to sing softly to himself. The song was simultaneously beautiful and terrifying, causing images to swim through my vision of existing in perfect light with countless other beings, then ripping away, falling, falling, falling into flame and darkness.

The song was filled with regret and above all a terrible malice that chilled my soul and my ragged flesh. The very temperature in the room dropped as he sang and our breath became visible as we exhaled.

I don't think he sang for us, or even knew he was doing it. After a long time, he stopped and finally faced Morgan.

"Do you know what you could have been if He'd protected you before?"

Morgan flinched at the mention of his death. It was the one subject we never talked about.

"That's right, Morgan." Satan's velvety voice gave me chills. "I know all about the mugging in the alley. Such a shame to have lost your life for the paper in your pocket."

His back was to me as he faced Morgan, but his head tilted to the side in a jerky movement, almost as if he wasn't used to making the simplest of gestures and was imitating another being instead.

"Do you know what you would have accomplished had He

sent his angels to protect you instead?" Satan continued spewing his lies, "You would have been one of the greatest athletes your country had ever seen. You would have had it all. Wealth, fame, power. You were stripped of all those glories along with your life that night. Where's the fairness in that? Where's the justice? You think your God is good and merciful? What is good or merciful about striking down someone on the cusp of greatness? Perhaps He worried that if He didn't allow your death, He'd eventually lose your love? Why serve a God like that?"

Satan stood in front of Morgan as he spoke, softly and confidentially as a friend, someone who understood the man's sorrow. Then, he laid a hand gently on Morgan's shoulder.

"And now look at you. Worse off than you ever were before, and where is He? Do you think he doesn't know exactly where you are? That paltry attempt at a rescue was simply for show to keep the other slaves in line. What I'm offering you now is a chance to truly be free. Be free of your bondage to a careless God —one who has only brought misery to your door. Instead you have a chance to be your own master, and join my ranks."

"I will never leave you nor forsake you," a gentle voice whispered in my ear.

I wanted to yell at Morgan to resist the lies even as my body begged me to give in. With what little strength I possessed, I pulled at the chains binding my wrists, hoping that the noise would draw Morgan's attention.

Part of the plan worked. Morgan's eyes slowly left the face of evil incarnate and drifted to mine. But what I saw in them grieved my soul. And a shadow rose between us, cutting off my view of my friend, and I knew at that very moment, he was lost.

———

I watched day after day as Morgan's body grew stronger from the hate against our Creator that he let consume him. It was a slow transition. Satan continued his daily visits to pump Morgan full of lies. And the more Morgan swallowed, the healthier he looked. But his renewed vitality was only on the surface, for inside my friend's soul had surely begun to rot and twist into something as grotesque as the rest of Satan's minions.

My resistance was rewarded with further torture. With each new demon feeding, my body weakened past the point I'd thought possible. And rather than having a companion in Morgan, I now had another manipulator urging me to give in to the darkness as he had done.

He'd tell me how much stronger he felt. He'd even hinted at something inside of him transforming. Until the day came when the change he'd spoken of manifested into something tangible.

Still chained to the pipes as I was, I watched his eyes move back and forth over the dank basement floor as the shadows followed his unspoken commands. It was like observing a macabre dance as he learned to master his new skill. It was horrifying, but I found myself fascinated even as my chest ached with the proof of the depths my friend had sunk into darkness.

I had completely lost track of time. The feedings were no longer helping me gauge the days that passed. In my misery, there were times I'd believed I'd always existed in this hell. The day came when I woke and Morgan was no longer strung up across from me, but standing tall, wearing a new type of armor—coverings that blended with the very shadows around us.

"I'm finally free," he said. They were the first clear words he'd spoken to me since our capture. "Logan, don't you understand, we've been fighting the war from the wrong side all along."

I could do nothing but weakly shake my head at him. There

was a fever in his voice that hadn't been present before. Where there used to be joy, I only heard anger.

"If you let go, the pain will stop. You'll be a new man. A better man than you ever were before. A more powerful one as well. Look," he stretched out his arm and called the darkness to himself. It covered his hand and then slid up his bicep until it looked like his arm from shoulder to fingertips had simply disappeared.

I looked into Morgan's eyes with disbelief. He'd not only fully given up on himself, but on our beloved Creator. And for what? A cool party trick?

I woke to a blinding pain in my shoulders, but for once it wasn't from a demon bite. One arm hung limp and useless by my side. There was a good chance both shoulders were dislocated from being stretched apart and taking the brunt of my full body weight for so long. Sensation in my hands was almost non-existent, only a slight tingling feeling remained. That was a small mercy.

I turned my head and watched with half-lidded eyes as Morgan moved to my other arm and started to unfasten the chains that held me in place. My shoulder was screaming now as it bore all my weight. I'd long since lost the ability to stand on my own.

Morgan wrapped a steady arm around my waist as he freed my hand and then staggered under the dead weight of my body. My raw and torn flesh shot jolts of pain throughout my being with every jostling movement as he lowered me to the floor—but it was nothing compared to the agony in my shoulder joints.

What was happening right now? Was he setting me free? Was his surrender to Satan all a ploy to free the both of us?

My logical mind strained to snap the pieces together, but it was sluggish after weeks of torture and lack of sustenance. I struggled to shake the cobwebs from my brain, but they'd been there so long I feared they'd now taken up permanent residence.

"I'm gonna put those shoulders back in their right place, mate," he sounded more like the Morgan I knew, but what if this was a trick? "I'm not going to lie to you, it's going to hurt like the dickens, but it needs to be done. You ready?"

I managed a wobbly head-bob, which resembled a nod.

"Alright, I'm gonna lay you on your back to do this."

He lowered my torso to the floor with zero help from me. Once I was splayed out on the grimy basement floor, Morgan grabbed my right wrist and slowly pulled on my arm. I gritted my teeth through the intense, searing pain.

Morgan's face pinched with concentration and exertion as he continued to pull my arm away from my body, standing to get better leverage. An eternity later, there was a clunk as the bone slid back into place and although still incredibly sore, there was a lessening of pain from that shoulder.

"One down, one to go. You still with me, mate?" Morgan asked.

"Yes," I managed to rasp through my dry throat and parched lips.

He nodded and took hold of my left wrist, repeating the agonizingly slow process again until I heard the familiar clunk of the bone being reset followed immediately by the same relief I'd felt from the previous side.

I wiggled my fingers as sensation flooded back into my arms. Morgan helped me up to a sitting position.

My throat worked to swallow, but nothing happened because of the absence of moisture. I fastened my eyes on Morgan and croaked out a single word, hoping he knew what I was trying to say.

"Escaping?"

Morgan's eyes blazed and his mouth set in a hard line.

"No. That's not why I unchained you. We both know you're too weak to go anywhere right now. I wanted to talk to you about why you should join forces with us."

My stomach turned. Had there been any food in it, I would have thrown it up.

Morgan wasn't here to orchestrate our escape, even though he was now in a position to do so. He was here to try and talk me into turning my back on our Creator.

"Satan was right," Morgan was saying, "Where was God and His army when we needed Him? Satan did this to us to show us the truth. To set us free."

I shook my head. Incapable of having a real conversation with him, it was the only way I could communicate. Satan wasn't trying to set us free, he was using us to grow his own army.

I wouldn't lie to myself and say my faith hadn't been shaken by this experience, but I wasn't willing to sell my soul for freedom.

"I am here," a voice whispered in my head.

Morgan droned on and on and at some point I just blankly stared back, not hearing anything that was coming out of his mouth. Eventually he realized I wasn't paying attention to him. He grabbed my sore shoulders and shook me roughly.

"Wake up!" he yelled in my face. His own features had turned red and were now filled with rage. Nothing about that was from our Father. Was it too late for Morgan? "The Creator doesn't care about you. He doesn't care about any of us. We're all a big joke to Him. Pawns to move around His chess board while He's bored."

A rage filled me like I'd never experienced. It bubbled up from my chest and shot down my arms.

That wasn't the Truth.

No matter the amount of abuse Morgan or Satan or his demons dished out, it was on *their* heads, not our Creator's.

The maddening anger that filled my soul at Morgan's words burst from me all at once, and with a shout I threw my arms up to dislodge his hold on me, shoving him back with both hands.

Morgan flew across the room as twin bolts of blue and white light shot from my palms and hit him in the chest. A crackling sensation weaved over my fingers as I looked down at the remnants of whatever power I had wielded.

Hunters didn't have abilities like this.

When the sensation and light disappeared from my hands, I jerked my head to gape at Morgan. There was a charred hole in his armor—right in the middle of his chest. He shook his head once and returned my stare with wide eyes.

Then a slow grin appeared on his lips.

———

Author Commentary: Chapter 9
JulieHallAuthor.com/logan-9

*M*organ's hurried steps echoed as he ran up the basement stairs, no doubt rushing to report that I'd finally snapped.

I stared down at my hands in horror.

What had I just done?

My rage against Morgan's words had fueled some power inside me and now the floodgates were open.

Hunters don't have powers like this, I repeated to myself.

Would I even be allowed back in the heavenly realm now? This power had to have sprung from evil, didn't it? A result of my long weeks being linked with demon-kind? It had burst forth in a fit of blinding fury.

"Run."

That whispered voice in my head snapped me back to attention. The adrenaline pumping through my veins afforded me a moment of mental clarity.

Now was my chance. Morgan had freed me from my chains and had run from the basement, leaving me completely alone.

Whether it was an oversight on his part, or simply an assumption that I didn't have enough strength to move, I didn't know.

And I didn't care.

I gathered every bit of strength I had and pushed myself to my feet. I wobbled before being able to take a step toward freedom. Grinding my teeth together, I set my mind on a single endeavor: leaving this wretched basement of horrors behind.

One step turned into two and eventually I'd made it to the stairs. I used the handrails, despite the objection of my recently relocated shoulders, to push and pull myself to freedom.

I stopped at the top of the landing and listened for any noises. For all I knew there could be a horde of demons camped out in and around the house. But time was a luxury I didn't have.

After waiting thirty seconds without hearing the scrape of a claw on the floor, or the shrieking chirp they used to communicate, I slowly opened the door.

My eyes darted around the empty room, expecting a creature, or even Satan himself, to materialize at any moment. I paused momentarily, then—with a spurt of energy—I stumbled to the front door and pushed out into the open air.

My eyes watered at brightness they were no longer accustomed to, but I couldn't wait for the temporary blindness to cease. I lurched forward, tripping and rolling down the few steps to the ground.

I hit the packed dirt with one of my injured shoulders and a bolt of pain lanced through my body. An anguished cry burst free.

Forcing myself to my feet once again, I ran into the forest surrounding the prison I'd just escaped, stumbling repeatedly as I fled.

Weaving around foliage and trees, I almost ran right into a demon before skidding to a stop.

It turned on me with an otherworldly snarl.

I had nothing to defend myself with. They'd deprived us of our weapons before I'd even awakened to find myself chained to those awful pipes.

Oh, Father, please help me.

The creature charged and I held up my hands in defense, sure they were going to be sliced from my arms at any moment. But the strange power I'd exercised against Morgan sprang to life once again, hitting the demon square in its middle and immediately stopping its forward momentum.

I kept my hands outstretched and watched in morbid, detached fascination as the demon let out a final shriek and its body shook as if electrocuted. Is that what I was doing? Electrocuting it?

Finally, the demon's appendages folded in as if every muscle was contracting at once. And then it stopped moving. Several heartbeats passed, and the creature's corpse turned into a pile of ash.

Bile churned in my stomach as I stared at my defeated foe. I should be running. I knew that, but I was frozen.

Something sliced into my back from shoulder to waist, splitting the flesh and muscle and allowing blood to flow freely down my spine.

This wasn't over.

I barely had time to turn before the demon was on me. Its teeth snapped, inches from my face. I pushed back with my hands, but my strength had left me. It was just about to bite into my neck when the lightning shot from my palms once more, and sent the creature flying off me, crashing into a nearby tree.

It screamed its outrage and came rushing at me again. I lifted my hands and found the power inside to blast the demon just as I had done with the last one. After the beast dissolved into smoke and ash, I didn't linger.

I turned and fled.

I ran, stumbled, and even crawled as far as I could until my body finally gave out on me somewhere in the middle of the wooded area. Only then did I sink into darkness once again.

———

"I said back up!" boomed a voice.

I winced at both the volume and the brightness behind my closed lids.

"I think he's waking up." This voice was softer.

"Do you think he's going to be weirded out that we're all just staring at him?" That sounded an awful lot like Kevin, but how could that be when I was trapped in the basement dungeon of that old house? That didn't make sense either because there was no light in the hovel I'd been surviving in for weeks.

I tried to open my eyes, but they were weighted down by lead.

"Seriously, he's waking up. We should listen to Alrik and back up."

Kaitlin.

How were my friends here? Where was I?

I wasn't going to find out until I pried my lids open.

It took a bit of effort and time stretched. My friends must have held their breaths, because when I finally managed to wrench my eyes open, a collective whoosh of air sounded. I viewed the room around me through the screen of my lashes.

"Oh, thank goodness you're awake." Kaitlin threw herself at me and began to cry. The force of her sobs shook the bed. I winced at her weight on top of my sore body, but held back the groan.

"Woman, get off of him," Alrik barked. "Can't you tell the poor guy is in pain?"

"Oh, my gosh," Kaitlin scrambled off of me and jumped from the bed as if it were on fire. "Logan, I'm so sorry. I'm just so happy that you're back. And okay-ish," her features pinched, "*Are you okay?*"

"Yeah, of course." That probably wasn't an honest answer, but what else was I supposed to say?

"What happened to you, man?" Kevin asked timidly. His brows pulled together, "We've been looking for you and Morgan for weeks. It's like you just . . . disappeared."

I took a deep breath. Overwhelmed, but trying to hide it.

"I think I should talk to one of the superiors about what went down first."

"Oh, yeah, right. Of course." Kevin nodded his agreement, but it was simply a tactic to prolong the inevitable.

If I could go the rest of my existence without having to relive the last few weeks in any way, shape or form, I would. But people were going to want to know what had happened. It wasn't something I wanted to talk to my friends about right now. Or ever for that matter, but especially not right now.

Everything was too raw. My mind—along with my body— was damaged beyond my friends' comprehension. And then there was the problem of my new power. I didn't know what it meant. And as hard as it was to admit—even to myself—I wasn't sure I wanted the truth.

Things were different now. I had changed in that dark basement. And I wasn't sure if I'd ever be the same person again.

———

Author Commentary: Chapter 10

JulieHallAuthor.com/logan-10

CHAPTER 11

"*You're* joking, right?" The look I shot Shannon was ice cold. Because of the extensive damage that was done to my body, a week later I was still in a room at the healing center, our realm's version of a hospital.

All I wanted to do was go home and sleep in my own bed—just one night—and then get back to training. But I'd been temporarily benched.

Didn't they realize I needed to get back to a normal routine?

"I'm afraid not, Logan. Considering what you went through, it's absolutely mandatory for you to talk with someone before we reactivate your status as a hunter." She delivered her short speech with the same tone she did everything, but there was a glimmer in her eye I didn't like. It looked an awful lot like pity.

"This is ridiculous." I crossed my arms over my chest and refused to make eye contact. Instead, I stared at the white wall in front of me. Whoever thought white was soothing was an idiot. The urge to punch my fist through the wall hit me hard and fast. I wiped a hand down my face instead.

"Logan." The softening of her voice startled me into looking at her. Her face remained stoic, but I had never heard compassion like this in Shannon's voice before. "You've been through an ordeal that very few people have ever experienced. Thank the Lord for that. You'd need therapy even if only half of the things you listed in your report happened. But I would still insist you seek counseling for the wounds we can't see."

I pressed my lips together tightly, knowing exactly what she was referring to. They were basically expecting me to go crazy at any moment. And they didn't even know about my new ability. I'd left that out of all my reports, written and verbal.

"With everything you've gone through, it's a miracle you're healing as well as you are." She gestured to my body, which at this point was devoid of all the visible scars that had been inflicted on me during my captivity.

My friends knew nothing about the three long, angry wounds running across my back that hadn't healed. I'd spotted them in the mirror the night before. So, no matter how *well* I looked on the outside, until those disfigurements healed, it meant that I still carried the mental scars of my torture as well.

That's just the way things worked around here. Our physical scars were a manifestation of emotions or experiences we hadn't fully recovered from.

There was no way for me to hide those marks from the healers who came in to treat me. Shannon, being part of the hierarchy of hunters, most likely had been informed of them as well. Thus, I was being sent to the realm's equivalent of a shrink to talk about my . . . *feelings*.

My lip curled at the thought of sitting down and openly talking about the conflicting emotions churning around inside me. I'd much rather work my issues out on a punching bag, practice dummy, or sparring partner.

"Physically speaking, you could be ready to go back to training with a few days' more rest."

Correction, I was ready to go back two days ago.

"But your mental state is just as important to us."

I refused to engage her in conversation anymore.

"Logan," there was that softened voice again. I hated it, "you were held captive and tortured for six weeks straight."

Keep your expression neutral. Don't show any emotion.

"You haven't spoken a word about Morgan since we retrieved you from Earth. We only know what happened to him from your written reports. What happened was awful. The reality of the situation is that you need to heal more than just your body. I'm sorry you don't like the idea, but if you want to remain a hunter, this is the only way to do it. Otherwise we'll be forced to find a different position for you."

At that last comment, I jerked my gaze to her.

They were considering reassigning me to a different job? She read the question and fury in my eyes.

"Don't let that happen. Keep fighting."

Without any fanfare, she turned on her heel and walked from the room.

Squeezing my eyes shut, I pinched the bridge of my nose. Would this nightmare ever end? I guess this meant that I was going to get my head shrunk.

———

I felt like a voyeur as I watched through the doorway as the couple embraced. The man and woman looked to be somewhere in their forties, but honestly, I wasn't that good at judging age. He leaned down and whispered something in her ear, and she giggled.

It was strange to watch a grown woman giggle. She nodded at whatever he'd said to her and then went on her toes to place a chaste kiss on his lips. They finally broke apart and I stepped back from the doorway, pretending to find something on the opposite wall really interesting.

"I'll see you for dinner, sweetheart," the man called back over his shoulder before leaving the room and continuing down the hallway. He passed in front of me and offered a smile and small nod of his head.

"You can come in now, Mr. London."

Totally busted.

I schooled my features into the hardened mask I'd been perfecting ever since being captured by Satan and his demons, and strode into the room. The woman was now seated behind her desk, so I picked a chair and sat—waiting for her to speak.

I didn't have anything to say.

Those scars on your back tell a different story, my mind whispered to me.

"Hello, I'm Deborah. May I call you Logan?"

I nodded.

"Wonderful," she smiled, and it lit up her whole face. It was still hard to make out her age. Her silver hair was pulled back in a twisty thing, but rather than looking grey from age, it shone with vitality. Her face had some fine lines, but it added interest to her appearance.

Why was I bothering to even try to nail down her age in a realm where appearances meant very little? Oh right, because it distracted me from why I was here to begin with.

When I didn't respond, she pushed on undeterred.

"So, Logan, tell me about yourself."

On her desk, I spied a folder with my name written clearly across it. I looked at it pointedly and then up at her.

"Don't you already know everything about me?"

"Do you really think you can get to know someone by reading a small list of facts about their life and afterlife?"

Touché.

I sighed. If this is what I had to do to get back to being an active hunter, I guess I was going to have to grin and bear it.

Leaning back in the chair, I folded my arms across my chest. "Fine. Where would you like me to start?"

"How about your earliest memory? And we'll go from there."

An abrupt laugh burst out of me, "Are you serious? You want to hear my whole life story?"

She leaned forward in her chair with a gleam in her eye, "Oh no, Logan, I want to know so much more than that."

———

"You're messing with me right now, aren't you? She actually drove a tent peg through his head?"

Lapidoth laughed at the look of shock on my face, "I promise, I'm telling the truth. And as you can imagine, it was a big deal back then to be taken out by a woman. Barak had won the day, but the glory went to another. And to think it was all because he wouldn't go into battle without her. Ha! Served him right. My Deborah is always right."

"What are you two talking about out there?" Deborah called from within her office.

Lapidoth poked his head around the corner, "Just some of the highlights from the glory days, dear. All good things."

"Well, don't scare the poor boy, LD. Times were different then."

"Should I be more offended that she referred to me as a boy, or that she suggested your story would scare me?"

Lapidoth chuckled and moved out of the way so I could enter Deborah's office. "My advice is to ignore her comment altogether."

"I heard that," Deborah yelled back to her other half from behind her desk. I took my usual chair just as he shouted, "I know," from what was probably the end of the hall.

Deborah smiled showing the playfulness of their relationship, "What am I going to do with that man?"

"For as many years as you've had together, I'm pretty sure you have it figured out. You're putting on a show for my sake. And speaking of, I think we should reserve these little meetings to talk about your life instead of mine. You've obviously led a more interesting existence than I have, so I don't understand why we're wasting our time discussing me."

She rolled her eyes.

Deborah rarely talked about herself during our sessions. But Lapidoth—LD for short—was usually here before my appointment and we'd fallen into a somewhat friendly acquaintance. He was always ready to brag about his wife and I'd learned quickly he had every right to do so. At one time, the woman had actually been the leader of Israel. Way back in ancient times before they even had official rulers. We're talking many millennia ago.

When I'd joked about her having been a queen she corrected me and said that she was a Judge during that time. And then, with a soft smile on her face, she'd rolled her eyes at me.

They were a hard pair not to like.

After three months, I was finally not dreading these sessions. Although my scars still hadn't disappeared. The one time I brought it up, Deborah waved it off, telling me some things just took time, and other things were all about the right timing.

"So, today will be our last session."

My eyebrows shot up so far they hid behind hair I'd let grow too long.

I'd gone back to training a couple of months ago, but it was under the strict understanding that I still wasn't cleared for active missions.

"Does this mean . . . ?" It was almost too much to hope for. If I was done with my counseling, that meant they'd made a decision about my status as a hunter.

I'd leaned forward in my chair without realizing it—my hands white-knuckling her desk.

Her smile widened and she nodded. "Yes, Logan. You've been cleared to get back into active duty as a hunter," she reached across the desk to pat the fingers that were probably leaving indents in her wooden desk, "I know the scars are still there, but—"

Deborah's words cut off abruptly the moment her hand touched mine. Her eyes widened and she sucked in a sharp breath of air.

"Deborah?" Her eyes stared right through me and a pained look pinched her features before smoothing out again. "Deborah?" I asked again, forcefully removing my hand from beneath hers.

Her strange spaced-out look was as disturbing as her touch. Skin-to-skin contact meant the empathy link sprang to life. Sharing emotions when we touched is a part of this new existence that I have always been uncomfortable with. Now I hated it because it instantly brought back memories of my captivity, and thoughts of the time spent in that dank basement were coupled with dark emotions I didn't want to share with anyone else.

When Deborah's hand had landed on mine, her happiness had pushed into me, but that emotion was quickly swept away by a strong feeling of shock.

"What just happened?" I demanded.

"You'll figure it out." Her voice had taken on a monotone quality that frankly, was just plain freaky.

"Figure *what* out?" I demanded.

She continued as if I hadn't spoken. No longer staring through me, her eyes seared into my own, "This existence isn't going to be what you expected. Your time here is only *part* of the journey. It may take a while to get there, and there are times ahead that are going to be harder than you've ever experienced, but in the end, you'll make the right decisions and figure it out. Don't run from your purpose. Embrace everything you'll learn, and use it to continue your journey. It will be worth it. *She* will be worth it."

"What the heck are you talking about?" I slammed back into the chair so fast it rocked on two legs before settling to the ground with a thud.

The noise made her jump, and then she blinked a few times. The intensity left her gaze, but a frown still marred her face.

"What's going on right now?" I demanded. Nothing like this had ever happened in our sessions before.

"Calm down, Logan." Deborah held both hands up in front of her in an attempt to pacify me. At least she seemed to be back to herself at this point.

"Are you done speaking to me in Chinese proverbs?"

Deborah's lips pressed together and her nostrils flared. She took a deep breath.

"I'm sorry about that. Let's wrap up this last session. What I said a moment ago . . ." she paused and I leaned even further away from her, "Well, we can discuss that another time. Right now, you just need to figure out who it is you want to be, and what it's going to take to get there."

"Is that what you meant when you told me I'd figure it out?"

She stared at me in silence for an uncomfortably long time before answering, "In part. But for now, let's see you get back into your normal routine, and go from there. I'm always here if you want to talk."

That wasn't likely to happen. Especially after what had just gone down.

She went on as if knowing my thoughts, "You don't think that day will come, but it may." She lifted her hand and gestured to the door.

I sat in stunned silence until it dawned on me that I was being dismissed. Deborah had never acted this way before. And to do so during our last session was even more bizarre.

"Okay. I guess I'll just get going now."

She nodded and a small smile appeared on her face, "This won't be the last I see of you, Logan."

I simply waved as I walked out the door. What else was I supposed to say to someone I respected, but who I hoped I never had a reason to meet again? Especially after the wacky sendoff she'd just given me.

Not paying attention to where I was going, I almost ran into LD a few doors down from Deborah's office.

"Oh, sorry man," I said and started to step around him. He mirrored my movements. I looked up at him with a question in my eyes.

"She wasn't only a Judge," LD's face was as serious as I'd ever seen it, "She's a prophetess too."

At my blank look, he continued. It's obvious he'd caught the last few minutes of our conversation, although why he was creeping in the hallway was a mystery to me.

"She sometimes still has visions, and is never wrong. What she said to you might not make sense now, but I believe someday it will. And know that her words were meant to encourage and strengthen you for your journey."

This was, by far, the strangest day I'd experienced in the afterlife. And that was saying something.

LD clapped me on the shoulder, gave it a gentle squeeze followed by an encouraging smile, and slipped into his wife's office.

"Hi sweetheart! I forgot to leave this with you. I know you wanted . . ." His voice faded as I walked down the hall, each step taking me further from them.

If Deborah was right, and what lay ahead was worse than what I'd already gone through, I'm not sure this was a journey I wanted to take.

———

Author Commentary: Chapter 11
JulieHallAuthor.com/logan-11

CHAPTER 12

*T*hree months had passed since I walked out of Deborah's office. I'd gotten back into the routine of being a hunter. I'd had several dozen successful missions to Earth. The afterlife was just beginning to settle back into place. And now this.

I had tried my best over the months to push Deborah's words —her prophecy—from my mind. But after doing some digging and finding out that the prophetess stuff was legit . . . well . . . that will mess with any guy's head.

Staring down at the sleeping beauty at my feet, I couldn't stop the last part of her cryptic message from floating to me. *She will be worth it.*

I shoved a hand in my hair and fisted the strands. What could the Creator be thinking? I didn't need this added complication.

I released my hair and with a frustrated growl stomped closer to the figure lying crumpled on the dirty mat. I crouched down to get a closer look at her.

Her mass of hair was everywhere, blocking my view of her

face. Gingerly reaching out, I pulled some of it back to get a better look at her.

She'd fallen on her side, her head tilted toward the ceiling. With her hair out of the way, I had a perfect view of her face.

Man, I was starting to feel like a creeper. I should probably wake her up or something.

As if it had a mind of its own, my hand moved towards her cheek. The moment my fingers brushed her soft flesh, sparks of electricity—the same power I'd used on Earth to escape from captivity—encased my hand and I jerked it away.

Amazingly, she appeared unharmed. Still passed out, but no charred holes in her—which was good.

I stared down at my hand as if it wasn't my own. The last vestiges of light were blinking out.

What just happened?

My heart pounded in my chest. It had been six months since I'd escaped Satan. When the new power to shoot lightning or electricity from my hands hadn't reappeared, I'd thought it was gone for good.

Maybe heightened emotions brought it on?

It's the one thing about my captivity I'd never told anyone. I'd let people believe I had escaped when Morgan's guard had been down. I hadn't brought it up to Deborah, or even any of my friends. I was ashamed that I'd somehow given in to the darkness and I just hoped that it hadn't damned my soul.

I had no idea what this meant, but it couldn't be good. I didn't want anything to do with this girl, but I didn't really have a choice in the matter. We were stuck together, whether we wanted to be or not. The sparks had to be a fluke.

I was truly a different person than the one who'd foolishly rushed into battle with Morgan that day. I had more control than this. I'd make sure I never used that power again.

No one had to know, especially not my new trainee. It was widely known I didn't like the empathy link, so it would be easy to keep from touching her.

A plan started to form in my head. One in which I would be able to train this newbie, and then we could both move on with our own afterlife . . . separately.

It was a while before I came back to myself and realized I needed to deal with her. I couldn't just leave her on the ground like that. I should like, flip her over or try to wake her up.

Taking a deep, calming breath, I tentatively reached out again, taking way too much time to try and figure out where to put my hands.

Waist was a safe zone, right?

I finally grasped her around her tiny middle, ignoring how fragile she felt in my arms as I began to lift and turn her over. Halfway through my maneuver the door behind me banged open.

I straight up dropped her. She landed sunny side down in a tangle of limbs. I spared her a quick wince before spinning around.

Yeah, way to go Logan. That didn't seem guilty or anything.

Shannon had walked back into the room, but had stopped just inside the entrance.

"What in the world did you do to her?" she asked, wide eyed.

"Nothing. I didn't do anything to her. If anything, this is your fault."

"Me?"

"Yeah, you didn't give her any prep for what we do. When I told her what the job was, she passed out cold."

"You didn't think to ease her into it, either?"

"Shannon, get real. I'm a dude. I wasn't about to hold her hand and give a watered-down version of her new reality," I glanced down at her, "I had no idea she would pass out, though. Do you think she does that a lot? Is that a girl thing?"

Shannon scoffed at me, then rolled her eyes.

What? That's a legit question.

"What are you doing back here, anyway?"

"I forgot to tell you where she will be living until she regains her memories."

Since she was my charge now, I should have thought of that already.

"Right. Big glass building?" That's where a lot of the temporary housing people lived.

"No. She'll be moving into the Redwoods."

I furrowed my brows, "Why did they stick her way out there?"

Shannon took a deep breath, "I don't know, Logan. Contrary to popular belief, I don't know everything. I'm just relaying what was told to me."

"But that's so secluded. Don't chicks need to be around other people or something . . . for socializing?"

She pinched the bridge of her nose, "First off, I'm pretty sure young ladies these days don't like to be referred to as *chicks.*"

I shrugged.

Shannon continued, "And I'm confident she'll figure out a way to socialize despite her living quarters. *You* do, after all, and you live out in that area as well," she cocked a perfectly-groomed black eyebrow at me, "Or is it that you don't like her that close to your cottage?"

"It's a cabin," I said through gritted teeth.

Shannon's lips pressed together and for a second I thought she might actually crack a smile. Then the moment passed. "Yes, of course. You're right. Well, now that you know where to take her, I'll leave you to it. I'm sure she'll wake up soon. Those who pass out from shock never stay down for long," she turned to leave.

"Wait!" I shouted before she escaped, "You never told me her name."

Shannon's brow creased as if she couldn't believe her own oversight, "Oh, her name is Audrey. And I can already tell you're going to have your hands full with that one."

As she strode from the room I stared down at the enchantress sprawled on the ground. The whispered words that escaped my lips were too quiet for even an angel to hear.

"You have no idea how right you are about that."

I had a feeling this Audrey girl was likely to be the end of me.

But maybe it wouldn't be a bad way to go.

———

Author Commentary: Chapter 12
JulieHallAuthor.com/logan-12

. . . and don't forget the blooper reel:
JulieHallAuthor.com/logan-bloopers

———

Thank you for reading *Logan*!
If you loved it, please write a review at
http://review.LoganBook.com

DEATH WAS ONLY THE BEGINNING

HUNTRESS

LIFE AFTER
BOOK ONE

JULIE HALL
USA TODAY BESTSELLING AUTHOR

HUNTRESS

LIFE AFTER

BOOK ONE

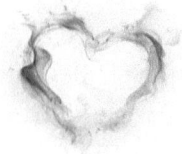

Death was only the beginning.

No one's afterlife is as dispiriting as Audrey's--at least that's what she believes after waking up dead without her memories and being promptly assigned to hunt demons for the rest of eternity.

She's convinced there's been a cosmic mistake; after all, she'd rather discuss the color of her nails than break them on angelic weapons. It doesn't help that her trainer, Logan, is as infuriating as he is attractive.

When an ancient weapon of unparalleled power chooses Audrey as its wielder, attracting the cautious gazes of her fellow hunters and the attention of Satan himself, Logan is the only one she can trust. With Satan's eyes now fixed on Audrey, a battle for the safety of the living looms in the shadows.

Fans of The Mortal Instruments, Supernatural, and This Present Darkness, won't want to miss this epic story of unfailing love and adventure.

EXCERPT FROM *HUNTRESS*
CHAPTER 3
THE JOB ETERNAL

Ten minutes later, Shannon held a door open for me as I stepped past her and into a room jammed full of people—and not just anyone. The room was packed wall-to-wall with huge, well-muscled guys! My stomach dropped. I'd been mistakenly drafted by the afterlife division of the NFL. This had to be a mistake.

Shannon placed a firm hand on my back and nudged me further into the room. I tried in vain not to gawk at the scene around me. Beefed-up guys sat conversing around twenty-five round tables. The atmosphere felt relaxed, almost like a break room. I couldn't pick up full conversations as we wove our way through the room, so my mind worked overtime inventing some of my own.

Hey man, what did you do today? the guy in the skintight purple T-shirt that said "I ROCK" on the front would say. And the dude on his left would answer in a deep, Schwarzenegger-esque accent, *I picked things up and put them down.*

We reached the other side without stopping to talk to anyone. Shannon placed her palm on the wall and produced another hidden door.

From my limited view behind Shannon's head, it appeared to be a gym of some kind. Not even the high-decibel manly noises coming from behind me drowned out the unmistakable sound of metal on metal. Shannon stepped to the side. That's when I saw, on the far end of the gym, two fighters locked in a death match. They were bearing down on each other so quickly I could hardly distinguish the movements. The source of the sound was the thick, heavy swords they were fighting with.

One of the fighters jumped high into the air and landed at least two body lengths from where he'd been standing, narrowly escaping a blow aimed at his shins. I gasped. A move like that wasn't humanly possible!

The fighters, wearing silvery, sleek body armor, didn't miss a beat as they bore down on each other with a series of quick blows. The movements blurred with their speed, the sound of the swords meeting deafening.

I gasped again when one of the opponents swung his sword in an arc and nearly took off the head of the other, who ducked and rolled just quickly enough to avoid decapitation. If this was a sparring session of some sort, it must have gotten out of hand. I looked up at Shannon anxiously. Surely someone should stop this!

Her face was a mask of calm, mixed perhaps with a bit of impatience. One of the fighters took advantage of an unsteady moment to get his opponent to one knee. He was just about to deliver a final blow when Shannon loudly cleared her throat. Both fighters froze. Shannon smiled coolly at them and said, "Logan, may I have a word with you?"

The fighter who had the advantage took a step back and lowered his sword.

"Sure, Shannon, just give me a sec," he said, not sounding nearly as out of breath as I thought he should. He reached an armored hand down to give his opponent a hand up. Not a bit of malice remained in their movements.

Logan shook the hand of his opponent, who was quite a bit bigger in both height and girth, and gave him a friendly pat on the back. They said something to each other I couldn't make out and chuckled before parting. The other guy gave Shannon a wave and a nod before pushing through a different set of doors.

As Logan moved toward us, his armor began to evaporate. First, his shin and shoe guards melted into the air, revealing brown sandals and dark-washed jeans. Then the metal covering his arms and hands disappeared, followed by his breastplate, uncovering a T-shirt that read "Hunters Rule, Demons Drool." He was leaner than the guys back in the break room, but still muscular. Last, his helmet evaporated. He looked younger than I expected . . . perhaps only a few years older than me. But who knew if age really meant anything here.

Shifting my weight I craned my neck to the left, trying to make sense of where his armor had just gone, peering around him as if it might magically appear somewhere behind him.

I was still gaping when he stopped a few feet short of Shannon and me. "Hey Shannon, what's up?"

He glanced my way with only a mildly curious look. I wasn't certain if I should be offended or relieved.

"Actually, I've brought you a new trainee."

Logan tilted his chin up to scan the area behind us. I turned my head as well to see who he was looking at.

"Oh yeah, that's great! Where is he?"

Shannon gave me a firm prod. Unprepared for the push and still gaping at Logan, I stumbled forward.

"Here *she* is," Shannon said with a smile.

Logan's eyes opened wider, and this time he *really* looked at me. He had dark blond hair, on the longer side and tousled, with wild highlights throughout, the type you get from too much time spent in the water and sun. His eyes started at my feet and slowly moved up my body until they locked with mine. Under the scrutiny, I registered that his eyes were a deep cobalt blue. It reminded me of the color of the ocean on a sunny day. The intensity of his stare embarrassed me. Heat rose to my face but was trapped in his gaze. I felt judged.

Without releasing my eyes, he addressed Shannon. His words came out deliberately, with an icy edge.

"You have got to be kidding me."

His tone sent a chill down my spine, which actually helped combat the warming of my cheeks. That was the final straw.

I broke his stare and pivoted on my heel. I'd had enough of all of this. Muttering to myself about how crazy this all was, I marched purposefully toward the door. I didn't care if there were a zillion muscle dudes on the other side, I just wanted out.

Before my fourth step, Shannon was in front of me. In fact, she appeared so quickly I walked right into her, bounced off, and landed on my butt. Dang, how'd she get there so fast? She appeared to be glowing but was no longer smiling. She looked over my head at Logan.

"You know we don't make mistakes about these things. There is a reason for this."

"She'll be eaten alive out there. Just look at her, Shannon."

Shannon glanced at me, sitting there on my butt, before looking back up at Logan. A shadow of doubt crossed her face but was gone almost as quickly as it had appeared. Eaten alive. How was that even possible when you were already dead?

"Logan, it is what it is. You've been chosen as her mentor. You need to train her as you would anyone else."

Neither of them spoke. I looked back and forth between the two. Then Logan asked with slightly narrowed eyes, "Is this because of what happened?"

Shannon's features softened perceptibly.

"No, Logan, this isn't some sort of punishment. You know things don't work like that here." Her voice was quiet but still strong when she continued, "What do you think they said about Romona when she first joined?"

Logan let out a deep sigh. There seemed to be some silent

communication, a faceoff, going on between those two. Shannon must have won, because after a few minutes her calm, cool smile returned.

"Thank you, Logan. I'll leave her with you now. You know what to do." The words sunk in fast as she turned to go.

"Wh-what?" My speech was stuttered as I scrambled up to stop her. In my rush I lost my footing again and ended up half-running, half-crawling after her. When the door shut behind her, it occurred to me how pathetic I must look. I struggled to my feet and stared at the door.

Indecision about whether to run after her or turn around and face my fate, kept me rooted in place. I was equally torn between wanting to shout at someone or break down crying. What in the world was going on? Whatever I might have thought the afterlife would look like, it surely wasn't this.

I inhaled a deep breath to steady myself. There was no use getting too upset until I found out what sort of job I had been assigned to anyway. Could it really be that bad?

So far, Logan hadn't made any attempt to talk to me. For all I knew, he wasn't even still there. I squeezed my eyes shut and let the air escape my lungs. When I opened them and turned, Logan was exactly where he had been when I attempted to make my grand exit. He was either giving me time or didn't know what to say, so I took control of the moment. At the very least, I needed to try to pull back some of the dignity I'd already lost.

I plopped my hands on my hips and let out a breath. "Okay, so will you at least tell me what exactly it is that we do?"

Logan looked me straight in the eyes and said, "We kill demons."

I saw his eyes, heard the words, and then everything went black.

Keep reading:
www.HuntressBook.com

Watch the HUNTRESS book trailer:
https://youtu.be/QkuzFdfKtR8

PLEASE WRITE A REVIEW

amazon   **good**reads

Reviews are the lifeblood of authors and your opinion will help others decide to read my books. If you want to see more from me, please leave a review.

Will you please write a review?
http://review.loganbook.com

Thank you for your help!

~ Julie

GET UPDATES FROM JULIE

JOIN MY NEWSLETTER

Please consider joining my exclusive email newsletter. You'll be notified as new books are available, get exclusive bonus scenes, previews, ridiculous videos, and you'll be eligible for special give-aways. Occasionally, you will see puppies. 🐶

Sign up for snarky funsies:
JulieHallAuthor.com/newsletter

I respect your privacy. No spam.
Unsubscribe anytime. 🤍

JOIN THE FAN CLUB

ON FACEBOOK

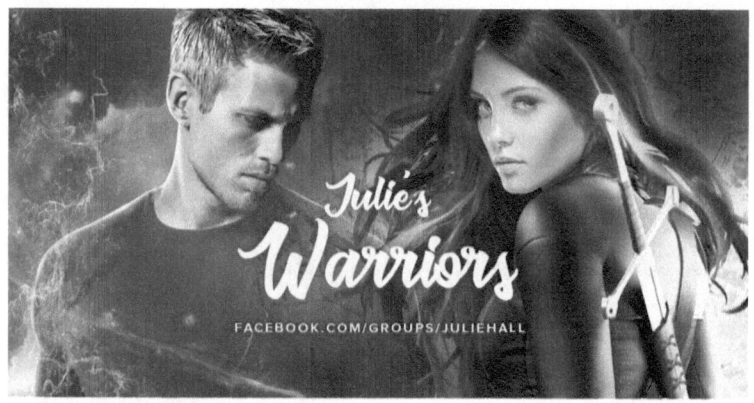

If you love my books, get involved and get exclusive sneak peeks before anyone else. Sometimes I even give out free puppies (#jokingnotjoking).

You'll get to know other passionate readers like you, and you'll get to know me better too! It'll be fun!

Join the Fan Club on Facebook:
facebook.com/groups/juliehall

See you in there!
~ Julie

ACKNOWLEDGMENTS

LOGAN would have never been a reality if I didn't have such amazing readers. It wasn't in my LIFE AFTER game plan to write this story, but like so much in life, it turned into a happy surprise. I am so excited to be able to bring to light Logan's story. Switching point-of-views was a stretching experience for me, but my readers had so many probing questions about the enigmatic and mysterious character, that I knew this story could only be told through his eyes.

I had some amazing help with LOGAN, so there are a few people I need to personally thank. The biggest hug of gratitude goes to my unbelievably supportive husband for not only allowing me to do this crazy author thing, but being the driving force behind all my writing. Even though it's my words on the page, we truly are a team and I couldn't--and wouldn't--want to do any of this without him.

I'd be lost without my funny, goofy, super hardworking, and lovable personal assistant, Amanda. Seriously, what would I do without you? Oh right, we already know I'd go insane. So with that hanging over your head, never leave me . . . or you'll be responsible for whatever dysfunctional existence I lead after if you do . . . but you know, *shrugs* no pressure.

Thank you LeAnn, Ashley, and Priscila for coming through for me on such short notice. Without you, who I consider to be not just loyal readers, but trusted friends, this book truly wouldn't have seen the light of day.

As always, thank you to my beta readers . . . the fabulous Robertson duo, who have had to suffer through every first rough draft I've created. You know I owe you big time. Beta reading is not a glamorous job. I hope to pay you back by helping you with your own stories someday. And yes, I'm going to keep putting that in my acknowledgements until it's a reality . . . so get on it!

I'd like to wrap up my thanks by coming full circle and thanking my readers. I truly have an amazing group of supportive and encouraging people who inspired me . . . *cough* pushed me *cough* . . . to write LOGAN. You who send me messages, leave reviews, and participate in my fan groups are the best. All my books are written with you in mind, but this one is dedicated to you. Without your feedback, I would have never thought to write it.

Lots of love!

ABOUT THE AUTHOR

JULIE HALL

My name is Julie Hall and I'm a *USA Today* bestselling, multiple award-winning author. I read and write YA paranormal / fantasy novels, love doodle dogs and drink Red Bull, but not necessarily in that order.

My daughter says my super power is sleeping all day and writing all night . . . and well, she wouldn't be wrong.

I believe novels are best enjoyed in community. As such, I want to hear from you! Please connect with me as I regularly give out sneak peeks, deleted scenes, prizes, and other freebies to my friends and newsletter subscribers.

Visit my website:
JulieHallAuthor.com

Get my other books:
amazon.com/author/julieghall

Join the Fan Club:
facebook.com/groups/juliehall

Get exclusive updates by email:
JulieHallAuthor.com/newsletter

Connect with me on:

[f] facebook.com/JulieHallAuthor

[BB] bookbub.com/authors/julie-hall-7c80af95-5dda-449a-8130-3e219d5b00ee

[g] goodreads.com/JulieHallAuthor

[o] instagram.com/Julie.Hall.Author

[▶] youtube.com/JulieHallAuthor

BOOKS BY JULIE HALL

Shadow Angel Series / ShadowAngelSeries.com

Fallen Legacies Series / FallenLegacies.com

Life After Series / LifeAfterBooks.com

AUDIOBOOKS BY JULIE HALL

Julie's books are also available on Audible!

http://Audio.JulieHallAuthor.com